LOSING IT

LOS

NG IT

ERIN FRY

Amazon Children's Publishing

Amazon Publishing
Attn: Amazon Children's Publishing
P.O. Box 400818
Las Vegas, NV 89149
www.amazon.com/amazonchildrenspublishing

Library of Congress Cataloging-in-Publication Data
Fry, Erin.
Losing it / by Erin Fry. — 1st ed.
p. cm.
Summary: Tired of being obese and reeling from his father's recent stroke, thirteen-year-old Bennett joins the cross country team to find out if there is more to life than French fries.
ISBN 978-0-7614-6220-0 (hardcover) — ISBN 978-0-7614-6222-4 (ebook)
[1. Obesity—Fiction. 2. Health—Fiction. 3. Cerebrovascular disease—Fiction. 4. Running—Fiction.] I. Title.
PZ7.F9223Fat 2012
[Fic]—dc23
2011032454

Book design by Becky Terhune
Editor: Marilyn Brigham

Printed in the United States of America (R)
First edition
10 9 8 7 6 5 4 3 2 1

To Zach, Jake, and Molly—
and to every young runner
who is not afraid to finish last

LOSING IT

CHAPTER 1
Belly Button Stains, Baseball, and 9-1-1

There's something about a belly button sweat stain that's just really gross. Like even worse than an armpit stain. I yank the front of my T-shirt away from the pudgy mound that is my stomach. I flap it a few times, hoping some air down there will make that little circle of sweat go away. No such luck. When I drop my shirt again, it immediately gloms onto that moist ring on my stomach.

I shrug. It's only Dad and me in the house, anyway. Like he's really going to care if my navel has perspiration issues.

It's a hot Saturday afternoon in August, a few weeks before I start eighth grade. Our wimpy window air conditioner is chugging away, barely pushing little puffs of cold air into our tiny family room. I've closed the blinds already, trying to block as much California sun as possible. We have an old fan from Dad's college days on full blast, but it's making more noise than cool air.

"You seen the remote?" I call out. I hunt around in the

couch cushions. Between the air conditioner and the fan, I need to crank up the volume on the TV if we hope to hear any of Vin Scully's voice.

"Look on top of the stereo!" Dad yells.

This means I have to stand up. Crap. With the room temperature at pretty much ungodly hot and my body resembling that of a walrus, pushing up off the couch requires a lot of grunting and more belly button sweat.

Ah, but there it is. The remote. That wonderful invention connecting us to the world and, more importantly, to baseball.

I flop back onto our couch and slosh a handful of fries through my shrinking puddle of ketchup. En route to my mouth, a big wallop of red lands on my T-shirt.

"Aw, man." I slap at the stain with a napkin. Thank God Dad said he'd take me back-to-school shopping soon. Most of my T-shirts are stained, faded, or too snug.

"You coming or what?" I call; but with a mouthful of fries, it comes out sounding like "Joo cubbing oh whuh?"

"Hang on, Bennett!" Dad hollers from the kitchen. "TV's not going anywhere!"

Dad was called in to work early this morning and wasn't home by game time. I had to set the DVR to record the Dodgers game. Even though the game started about an hour and a half ago, we'll fast-forward through commercials and probably catch up by the ninth inning. With Dad finally home from work, it's time to chill with the Dodgers and our "game" food: burgers and fries.

Dad huffs into the room, looking more tired than usual. He drops into his faded blue easy chair with a loud *humph*. He leans back and exhales, rubbing his temples with his thumbs.

He's been working a lot of overtime in the past few weeks. As a project manager for a construction company, he has to make sure all the guys on the job show up and do what they're supposed to. Today a crew that was digging trenches to lay some pipe hit a gas line, and the whole site was shut down. Sometimes Dad's job sucks. And lately it seems to really wipe him out.

Dad carefully stretches his left leg out in front of him and winces. He slowly rotates his swollen foot as if it's asleep.

"Leg bugging you?" I ask.

Dad grunts and leans over to grab his paper sack of fries. "I think it's the diabetes." He shakes his head. "Kept me awake all last night. Every time I moved, it was like someone poking my foot with a thousand pins." He leans back and sets his sock-clad feet on the coffee table. "Leg's kind of numb today."

His legs constantly go numb. Especially if he's been standing or walking a lot. But then, my dad's a big guy, and those legs are carrying a lot of weight.

I hit the button on the remote to unfreeze Dodgers pitcher Clayton Kershaw. He throws back his arm and, like poetry in motion, lets the ball fly in a perfect line toward the plate.

Ball. Inside. Crap.

I couldn't hit a baseball to save my life. It would take me the better part of an afternoon to huff around the bases, even if I could. But I love this sport. I have this dream of becoming a professional umpire someday. They have fat umpires, don't they?

My burger and fries are gone by the bottom of the second—as is any hope of a Dodgers lead. That idiot, dumb-bum Lowe, has pitched a six-run second inning that has Rockies fans celebrating at Coors Field.

In the bottom of the fourth inning, I let Dad fast-forward through the beer and car commercials while I gather our greasy trash and dump it in the kitchen. I grab a can of Coke from the fridge and swipe it across my forehead as I head back toward the living room. The cool aluminum feels really good. My butt hits the couch just as Dad unpauses the game.

Top of the fifth. Billingsley now pitching for the Dodgers.

"Kershaw's out, huh? Where's his curveball lately?" I ask Dad.

"Missing in action. Along with Matt Kemp's swing, I guess." Dad shakes his head. This is a sore subject with him.

"We're still in the running for the play-offs, though."

"Yeah, there's that." He closes his eyes for a second. "Man, I'm tired today." He rubs his temples again.

"You want some Tylenol or something?"

"No, just tired. These Dodgers aren't helping any, either."

The next few innings we don't talk much. That's kind of how it is at our house. If the Dodgers are having a really crappy game, Dad might gripe, but he usually doesn't raise his voice.

At the top of the sixth, the Dodgers have made up four of their six-run deficit. Dad's dozing on his throne, his head bobbing forward and then comically snapping back up with a snort. I can't help but smile at his double-chinned, Saturday afternoon bliss. These are definitely some of my favorite times: these lazy, baseball-watching afternoons. Baseball got my dad and me through my mom's death. It might sound like a dopey Hallmark commercial or something, but it's true. When baseball's on, we're both just good, you know?

My cell phone hums: P. G. I sigh. This can't be good.

"Yo," I say.

"You seen the game?"

P. G. is my closest friend, even though he's a die-hard Giants fan. The fact that he's calling leads me to believe that things aren't going to end well for my Dodgers. P. G. likes to rub it in when the Men in Blue suck.

"Watching it now, man."

"Ah, good," he says. "Call me when it's over." *Click*.

That's P. G. Man of few words. I drop my phone in my shorts pocket, lean back, and kick my feet up on the coffee table. I notice that there's still a sweaty ring around my belly button. Seriously?

I'm reaching for the remote to fast-forward us into the seventh inning when it hits me that my dad's snoring has stopped. In fact, looking over at him, it seems as if his breathing may have stopped, too.

My dad has this condition called sleep apnea. It causes him to stop breathing in his sleep pretty much every night. Still, I pause the game and quickly get up to switch off the fan and the air conditioner.

"Dad?" My voice is loud in the now-quiet room. "Dad! Wake up, man; it's almost the seventh-inning stretch! We gotta sing, right?"

His eyes pop open. Wide-eyed, he snorts a few times and blinks, like he's trying to focus.

"Ben . . ." His lips seem to have trouble moving. With the palm of his right hand, he pushes against his temple and squeezes his eyes shut. "My h-head. Call. Some. One."

I freeze halfway between the TV and my dad. My mind starts ping-ponging all over the place.

Call *who*?

Aunt Molly—my dad's sister in Vegas? She's a four-hour drive from Los Angeles, assuming there's no traffic—and it's Saturday, so no way is that gonna happen.

My dad's parents died before I even got a chance to know them. And my mom's mom, Grandma Jean? She's been in a nursing home for two years now, ever since she forgot to turn off a burner on the stove and nearly burned down her house. Every time I see her, she thinks I'm some paperboy named Willy who delivered newspapers to her house in, like, 1950. Who exactly am I supposed to call?

Then I get it. He means call an ambulance.

We have one cordless phone in our tiny, two-bedroom house. But it could be pretty much anywhere since both of us are famous for setting it down wherever we happen to be. I bolt toward the kitchen, saying, "Hang on, Dad. It'll be okay. Just breathe, okay?"

The cradle for the phone is empty. I curse quietly. I start zipping through the house, frantically looking in all the places our phone might be: kitchen counter, the nightstand next to my dad's bed, the shelf over the bathroom sink. Strike three.

From room to room I search, feeling my heart rate skyrocket and sweat start dripping down my cheek. I holler out, "I'll find it, Dad; don't worry!" and "Hang in there!" and "Just breathe!"

Panic is squeezing my throat. I have to keep swallowing. Hard. Where is that stupid phone?

Then, like a forgetful old man who can't find his reading glasses because they're on his head, I reach into my pocket. My cell phone. With shaking hands and short breaths, I flip it open and punch in 9-1-1. It takes forever to connect. I keep my eyes on my dad. He seems to be breathing. Barely.

"Nine-one-one, emergency response, how can I help you?"

"My dad, he's not breathing well. He says his head hurts. I think . . ." I try to push out the words without losing the cheeseburger I've just eaten. "I don't know. Something's wrong."

My own chest hurts suddenly. I can't seem to stand still. But my breathing is as labored as if I've just run a mile in PE. It's a struggle to keep the phone to my ear, my hand is shaking so badly.

"What's your address, hon?"

Without taking my eye off my dad, I mumble our address and cross street.

"Okay, hon, we've got an emergency crew on the way. I'm going to have you stay with your dad, and I'll walk you through what to do, all right?" The woman on the line pauses, waiting for me. But I'm swallowing fear so hard I can't answer. "Stay with me. Help is coming."

So I do. I wait. Every so often I check my dad's pulse as she instructs. She tells me to keep talking to him, even though his eyes are closed and he's not responding anymore.

"Hey, Dad, help is coming, all right?" I can feel a pulse in his neck. My hand is still shaking so much, though, that

I lose it and panic until I find his pulse again.

"We're going to be okay. Hang in there, Dad, please?" I keep staring at him, willing him to open his eyes and tell me he's fine: *It's just an attack of sleep apnea; flip the game back on, will you?*

But he doesn't. The seconds tick by at the speed of a sidewalk slug. I worry they've gone to the wrong house, that I've said the wrong address.

"They are coming to Twelfth Street, right? West Twelfth?"

"Yes, hon," she says evenly. "The ambulance is on its way. Should be arriving any second. Try to stay calm."

Stay calm? It isn't her dad slumped in this chair. It isn't her two fingers pressing against his neck so hard I'm afraid I'll pop through his skin. It isn't her heart beating five times faster than normal.

I've already lost a parent. I know that drill. If staying calm is going to help me keep this one alive, well, then, by all means I'll try to make it happen. But if the emergency crew doesn't get here soon, calm is about to go out the window.

Finally, I hear the distant sirens. When the flashing red lights reflect off the walls of our family room, I flip my phone closed. I fling open the front door, relief flooding through me. Finally, someone is here who can handle this.

Then as the guys with the stretcher barrel through my front door, my dad starts thrashing around in his chair.

As a fire engine pulls up in front of my house, its siren blaring, I see him try to stand up.

I yell, "Dad!" but my voice is drowned out by the screaming sirens.

Time slows down. I know that's not scientifically possible; but if you've lived through something like this, then you know exactly what I mean.

I see everything as if underwater. Magnified but blurry. The guys moving toward my father, shouting to one another. The Dodgers game still frozen on the TV. Dad's head now starting to loll to one side.

Through the open door I see Caleb Landen, the five-year-old across the street who I sometimes baby-sit. He buries his head in his dad's shoulder while Mr. Landen stares at our house.

Then, with no warning, my dad pitches forward. His body goes limp as he hits his head loudly on the coffee table.

And all hell breaks loose.

CHAPTER 2
Is Your Dad Dead?

Mr. and Mrs. Landen run over while Dad is being loaded into the ambulance. Caleb is wide-eyed, holding tight to his mom's hand. I understand. He's five. The exact age I was when I visited my mom in a hospital. Part of me thinks I should pat his little blond head, tell him it will be okay. But I'm too numb to do a whole lot of anything. And honestly? It wasn't okay when I was five. And it might not turn out okay now.

I remember, shortly before my fifth birthday, lying on the floor of my bedroom. I'd pulled out a calendar that had come in the mail with an ad for *Highlights* magazine. My mom came into my room as I was pulling off the cap of my red marker. She stood over me as I drew a lopsided *X* through the box for that day.

"Look, Mom!" I pointed. "Twenty more days. Then I'll be five." I flipped to the next page of the calendar and lifted it so she could see where I had circled April 12. "See?"

Her cheeks already had that sunken-in look. Her eyes were tired and heavy, though, at that point, no one knew why. My dad told me much later that he'd thought she was just an exhausted mom who needed more sleep. Or needed vitamins. Iron deficiency, my grandma declared. Nobody thought it was cancer. Or if they did, they didn't say it to me.

That day she sat on the edge of my bed, looking down at me and my *Highlights* calendar. Even though she looked worn-out, she was smiling the way a mom does sometimes when she's feeling lucky to be your mom. Maybe that's why I still remember the moment so clearly. It was probably the last time I saw that smile.

She leaned over and smoothed a piece of hair off my forehead, kissing the spot where it had been.

"Don't wish away the time, Ben-jo." She looked past me and out the window of my room. "It moves too quickly already without us marking it off."

I didn't get it then. All I wanted in the world was to be five. Five like Sammy, the cool kid at preschool with the cowboy boots. Kids started losing their teeth when they were five. I was going to get my training wheels off my bike when I was five.

Then, on a hot day in July, about three months after my birthday, I watched them lower my mom's coffin into the ground. I prayed with all my heart that I could get those Xed-out days back. Just two of them would have been great. A week of them would have been worth my autographed Tommy Lasorda baseball. I understood then about time. It was a gift. When it's gone, you can't get it back. I threw my *Highlights* calendar away a week later.

"Hey, Bennett," Mr. Landen says, shaking me from my thoughts. "Why don't I drive you to the hospital and stay until you can call another family member?"

What other family member? I'm thinking. *It's me and Dad. That's it.* But I just shrug and grab my cell phone and the house keys and climb into their cluttered minivan.

Before she shuts the passenger door, Mrs. Landen reaches in and squeezes my arm. I'm grateful that she doesn't try to tell me everything will be fine. Any kind words might bring on tears. Thirteen-year-old boys— even fat, easygoing ones like me—aren't supposed to cry in front of people. Especially fat, easygoing ones like me.

Caleb, however, doesn't get it. He stands there, clutching his mom's hand, and looks up at me thoughtfully.

"Hey, Bennett?" he asks before his mom can shut the door. "Is your dad dead?" His little face is squinched up, as if the thought of someone dead isn't necessarily a good thing but it could be interesting.

His mom tries to shush him. Actually, she looks like *she* might like to die.

"Bennett, I'm sorry. He's only . . ."

"Five," I interrupt softly. "Yeah, I know. I remember five." I look straight at Caleb, determined not to mess with him. "I don't know if my dad is dead," I answer slowly. "I hope not. I guess I'll have to go to the hospital and find out."

Something clicks in Caleb's brown eyes. "I hope he's not dead, Bennett." My chest burns with the same hope. "I really hope he's not."

I don't answer. I just shut the door to the van and look away as Mr. Landen hugs his wife and Caleb good-bye before hopping in with me.

Our short ride to the hospital is silent, except for the eighties rock playing softly on the radio. "Is there someone we should call? I mean, like a relative or something?" Mr. Landen asks as we pull into the hospital parking lot.

"My aunt, I guess." I've been mulling it over on the drive, and Aunt Laura is the only person I can think of. She isn't my first choice. She is simply my *only* choice. A heaviness—dread probably—settles deep in the pit of my stomach.

Our last meeting is still fresh in my mind, even though it was more than a year ago.

Aunt Laura had called my dad and asked if I could come over to celebrate my cousins' birthdays. Kiley and Josh were born the same month and often had a combined "family" party. It was clear to both Dad and me that my aunt had pretty much invited just me. Not my dad. But I didn't want to go in there alone. And Dad knew that.

As Dad pulled up to her house that day, eager to drop me off and get out of there, I turned on him. I was royally pissed off. "I can't believe you're going to drop me off and leave. This is so not cool, Dad."

"Ben . . ."

"Whatever," I said. But I couldn't resist one last jab. "I'm sure Mom would be thrilled at how you're reaching out to her sister like this."

Before he could answer, I slipped out and slammed the door behind me.

The next two hours sucked. Everybody treated me as if I were some poor, pitiful kid. They hugged me tightly and asked about my father, avoided any mention of Mom, and never really looked me in the eye. Then when the silence grew awkward, they patted my arm and walked away. Grandma Jean kept asking me for a copy of the newspaper or to find her cat, Jiffy, who had actually died two years earlier. My cousin Kiley—who is my age—was maybe the worst of all. When she saw me, she would look away, flash a wary half smile, and hurry off like my oversize belly was a disease and it might be contagious.

My cousin Josh was the only one who acted even remotely normal around me.

"Bennett? Want some cake?" he asked as the party was winding down and guests were heading toward the front door. I checked my watch. My dad was due back in fifteen minutes. Thank God.

"No, thanks." I didn't bother to tell him that I'd already finished off two slices.

"Want to come see my new Nintendo DS?"

"Naw, Josh," I said as gently as I could. "My dad's gonna be here soon."

"'Kay." He good-naturedly plopped down on the chair next to me.

Aunt Laura showed up a minute later.

"Josh, honey," she said, her voice all high-pitched and fake. "Why not take Bennett outside? Shoot some hoops with him or something?" She wiped her hands on her apron and looked at both of us like we should jump up and do it.

"Actually, my dad's coming any minute. I think I'll just wait for him here."

My aunt's eyebrows shot up. She pressed a finger to her lips, looking off to her left with this weird expression on her face.

"Josh, would you go make sure your grandma hasn't wandered off?"

Josh looked at me once quickly. His eyes seemed to say "Sorry, bro." He slid off his chair and headed toward the front door.

"Bennett," my aunt said softly, lowering herself to the empty chair, "your uncle and I are concerned about you."

My jaw tightened. I wouldn't look at her.

"You're alone so much, what with your dad working all that overtime. And your eating habits are . . . well, obviously unhealthy. There is no easy way to ask this, Bennett, but . . . is your dad taking care of you? Do you, you know, go to the dentist? See a doctor?"

My dad once told me that hate was not the opposite of love, since both are really strong emotions, making them more alike than different. But I can tell you, in that moment, I hated the woman sitting next to me.

I bit my bottom lip, struggling to find the courage to tell her to shut up and go away.

"Bennett, please understand . . ."

"I'm fine." I had to speak through my clenched teeth. "My dad is . . ." I thought about my dad and the way I'd talked to him before he left. "We're . . . I'm fine."

She opened her mouth but closed it again quickly. "Well, then. That's that."

She stood up. I prayed Dad would get there quickly.

"Your mother would have never . . ." She looked down at me. Her eyes were sad. "She would have hated seeing your dad like he is, and she wouldn't want to see you like this, Bennett. She'd want to know you were healthy, active, happy. I just don't think . . ."

I stood up and faced her, shaking from head to toe.

"How would you know what my mom would want?" I asked quietly. "She didn't even trust you enough to tell you that she was dying, did she? You have no clue what—"

"Bennett?" My dad's large frame filled the door to the living room. "You ready to go?"

My aunt took a quick step backward, away from me.

"Well, then, Bennett," she said loudly, pasting a smile on her face. "Thanks for coming."

"Yeah," I mumbled, and squeezed past my father,

ignoring Josh as he said his thanks and good-bye.

In the car, my dad and I didn't speak for a few minutes.

"You okay?" he asked finally as he made the turn onto our street.

"Yeah."

"Want to tell me what happened back there?"

"Just Aunt Laura being Aunt Laura." I hoped he would leave it alone.

He did.

But after that we didn't see my aunt or my cousins anymore. Aunt Laura never called to invite me over. And my dad didn't ask why.

• • •

Standing in the doorway of the ICU waiting area, Mr. Landen snaps his cell phone closed and clips it onto his belt.

"Therese says she finally got Caleb settled down."

He says this as if I've asked him a question. Then he leans back into the vinyl chair, trying to get comfortable. He should save himself the trouble; it won't work.

"He's worried that something's happened to you."

"Yeah." I look down at my shoes.

Something has *happened to me!* I want to yell. I watched my dad have a seizure or a heart attack or I don't know. Something. I don't know if he is alive or if he's— well, not alive.

But part of my brain, the part that isn't numb from shock, realizes that Mr. Landen is being a kind neighbor, stepping in because no one else is available. He has a five-year-old and a wife at home. Probably papers to grade, too—he's a teacher at the local college. I bet the last way he wants to spend his Saturday afternoon is at a hospital with me. I mean, come on, it's the last place I want to be.

After some awkward, silent minutes, Mr. Landen stands and stretches his long, skinny legs. He pushes his wire-rimmed glasses up his nose.

"Hey, Bennett," he says, smiling, trying to cover up the worry that's plainly showing in his eyes. "I'm going to go grab something from the cafeteria. Can I get you anything? A drink? A snack?"

We've been here at least two hours. My stomach, though, is too knotted to think about food. For once.

"I'm good, thanks."

Mr. Landen looks at me hard for a moment. He sighs and seems to make up his mind about something. Then he turns and walks out of the waiting room.

I have yet to see my dad or any doctor who can tell me what's going on. I know Dad was alive, barely, when he left our house; but that's it. For the eighteenth time I walk over to the receptionist. "Do you have any idea when I can see my dad?"

For the eighteenth time she smiles kindly and says, "Sorry, sweetie. The doctor will let me know when we have news."

Frustrated and anxious, with my tailbone throbbing

from sitting, I clench my fists and growl, "Uhhh!"

Her smile gets a little less bright. "I know it's hard to wait, but there isn't much we can do right now. Why don't you grab something to eat?"

I sigh and walk slowly back to my seat.

For whatever crazy reason, I think of my aunt then. The way she looked at me that day in her living room, accusing my father of neglecting me. I also think back to when I was five, the day of Mom's funeral. The day I tossed a handful of dirt into my mom's open grave. The day my dad and Aunt Laura had it out.

After the funeral, we went back to my house. Aunt Laura pulled me into her arms and hugged me tight—too tight. I stood there like a statue as she sobbed into my hair. She smelled like a rosebush. Or maybe sixty of them. Her shiny, pointy nails dug into my arms like thorns. My dad finally pried her off, saying gently, "Come on, Laura. He doesn't understand. Don't make it worse."

And then the fireworks started.

Aunt Laura swiped at her tears. Like a lioness ready to attack, she whipped around, her eyes blazing. "Don't make it worse?! How could it *be* any worse? How could you have let this happen, Paul?" she screamed.

The murmuring in our living room stopped, and everyone stared at us. Laura narrowed her eyes, accusing and hateful. My dad, protectively—and probably instinctively—moved his large frame in front of me.

"Laura." His shoulders sagged. "Not now. Please? Bennett—"

"It's Bennett I'm concerned about!" Tears ran down her cheeks again, smudging her makeup. She looked like a raccoon. An angry one. My uncle Jim appeared at her side. Desperately, he tried to hush her and lead her away. For the tall, thin woman my aunt is, though, she held her ground pretty firmly.

"You knew she was sick!" Aunt Laura spat, her hands clenched. "You knew and yet you kept it from us! From me! Her sister! She needed treatment, Paul. Drugs, chemo, a doctor who knew what he was doing. Not some idiot shoving herbs at her. How could you let her die?"

"Stop! That's enough, Laura!" My dad's voice, like I'd never heard it before, was as tight as my aunt's clenched fists. "Leah knew what she wanted and how she wanted to—handle things: her disease. She insisted I keep quiet until we knew if it was, uh, terminal. We told you as soon as we knew she wasn't going to make it. I respected her wishes. It was her life. What else could I do? What would you have done?"

"I'd have gotten her help!" Tears streamed down my aunt's face, and lines of clear snot ran from her nose. She swiped at them with the back of her hand. "I'd have cooked for her—healthy meals, not that fast-food junk you all eat—and made her take the stupid medicines. I wouldn't have just sat there and watched her die!"

Uncle Jim put his arm around her and tried to steer her away. He called to his kids that it was time to leave, to get in the car. Walking away, he glanced back at my dad apologetically, as if to say "Please don't hold this against her. She's not herself."

I don't think my dad even noticed. He just looked, I don't know, beaten.

My dad's sister, Aunt Molly, walked over and gently placed her hand on his shoulder; but my dad's head was down, and he didn't move. I squeezed his hand, hoping to comfort him and remind him that he still had me. He looked over and gave me a sad little smile. "It's okay, Benjo," he said softly. "We're going to be okay."

Apparently, Aunt Laura didn't think so. As my uncle led her out to their car, she turned back once more. Sobbing, she screamed, "I won't let you kill Bennett, too, Paul! I won't!"

Aunt Laura had gotten it wrong, though. He hadn't killed me. He'd killed himself.

CHAPTER 3
Waiting, Waiting, Waiting

By five thirty Aunt Laura hasn't arrived at the hospital yet, a fact that's beginning to irritate Mr. Landen, if his leg jiggling and watch checking are any indications. I think he wants to go home. He probably can't understand why she hasn't dropped everything to comfort me, her poor nephew.

Thankfully, P. G. and his family show up at the hospital about a half hour later. Mrs. Gomez swoops in immediately and pulls me into the biggest bear hug ever. The smell of cinnamon and onions washes over me. For a moment I feel sort of better. Mr. Gomez squeezes my shoulder and looks me right in the eye to ask, *"¿Cómo estás?"*

"I'm okay, Mr. Gomez. I just wish someone would tell me if my dad's all right. Nobody will tell me anything."

Mr. Gomez's eyes narrow. "We'll see about that, *mijo.*" He squares his shoulders, rises to his full height of five feet, four inches, and marches off.

Within thirty seconds he's over at the nurse's desk,

asking questions in both Spanish and English and waving his hands in all directions. Soon, they're both laughing. When I see her stand up and walk toward the ICU, I smile. For a short, balding, and rather round guy, Mr. Gomez is pretty good when it comes to getting people to do things.

P. G. has three sisters, all older than him. The two oldest are working today—both have jobs as hairdressers. But Selena, my favorite and easily the prettiest, is here. She flips the front of my hair and says, "Don't worry, Benito; your dad's tough. He's going to make it."

P. G. struts over like we're at school instead of in a hospital. He bobs his chin in greeting. "Hey."

"Man, am I glad to see you."

"It's been a day, eh, bro?" he asks.

"Yeah, you can say that again."

"You'll get some answers soon."

I hope so, but what if they're answers I don't want to hear?

The Gomez family goes nowhere without food. Sure enough, Mrs. Gomez pulls out a basket of hot, homemade chimichangas—deep-fried burritos that make my mouth incredibly happy—jalapeño corn bread, and soda. Mrs. Gomez only has to unwrap the first chimichanga. When the aroma hits me, I'm almost light-headed from hunger.

Mr. Landen splits, despite Mrs. Gomez's insistence that he sit and eat with us, saying he needs to hurry home. He makes me promise to call him when I hear anything. He, in turn, promises to keep an eye on our house, water the yard, bring in the mail, etc. There is a lot left unsaid, like when I might actually be back at that house to do it myself. But we don't go there.

Mr. Gomez must have threatened or bribed the admitting nurse. As I'm brushing the corn bread crumbs off my pants, a woman in blue scrubs comes to the door of the waiting room and looks down at her clipboard.

"Bennett Robinson?"

I stand up quickly, eager to finally know something. But then a feeling—fear? worry?—hits me. The two chimichangas now feel like six. The lights seem brighter and too hot. My butt tingles from sitting for so long. I look over at P. G. He tips his head slightly toward the nurse.

"Go on, man. Plate time."

He's right. It's time to get a move on, to step up to the plate.

"Want me to come with you, *mijo*?" Mr. Gomez asks.

"That's okay, Mr. Gomez. I'm good." But even as I say it, I know it's a lie. I'm about as far from good as Los Angeles is from China.

The nurse stands there tapping one long red fingernail on her clipboard, looking as if she has forty million other things to do besides wait for me to get my act together.

I clear my throat. "I'm Bennett."

"We've got some news about your dad. If you'll follow me, the doctor will . . ."

"Bennett!" someone shrieks.

All eyes turn toward the woman hurrying down the

hall in a perfectly matched jogging suit. Her arm is raised as if she's trying to flag down a taxi. Her reddish-blond curls are pulled back in a neat ponytail. Her white Nikes look as if they've never been worn before today. Under one arm she carries a hardcover book.

"Bennett!" Aunt Laura gushes, throwing her arms around me and touching her lips lightly to my forehead. "I'm so sorry it took me so long to get here!"

Both so's are drawn out dramatically. All she needs to do is wipe imaginary sweat from her brow like an actress in a really bad chick movie.

"Are you all right? How's your dad? How'd you get here?"

She holds me at arm's length and stares at me as if trying to see if I've been hurt in any way.

"Mrs. Robinson?" the nurse asks pointedly, wanting to get moving.

"No, no. I'm Bennett's aunt, not his mother," Aunt Laura corrects quickly, as if the lack of resemblance should be obvious. "And you are . . . ?"

"Busy," the nurse responds, clearly annoyed. "Now, if you'll excuse us for a second, I was about to take Bennett back, where a doctor can explain to him what's happening with his father."

The nurse starts to lead me away, but Aunt Laura stops her.

"I'm Bennett's closest relative. Which makes me

his current guardian," Aunt Laura declares. "I'll be accompanying Bennett."

The nurse's eyes narrow. "Where's Bennett's mother?"

Aunt Laura doesn't blink. "Deceased."

The nurse glances quickly at me. "And you're the designated guardian?"

Aunt Laura snorts. "I'm the only choice." She crosses her arms. "I mean, I don't know what Paul's will says. I don't even know if there *is* a will. But I'm here and I'm willing and, frankly, I'm all Bennett has."

Something resembling a punch hits my gut. I want to scream, *God, no! Anyone but her!* But it's as if my lips are frozen shut.

The nurse glances at her clipboard, then back up at my aunt. "There'll be papers that need to be signed. A social worker will take on the case and then you can work all that out. I guess for right now, though, you can come along."

The nurse swings her gaze toward me. "Is that all right with you?"

Seriously? I'd rather take a sharp stick in the eye, as my grandma used to say.

Mr. Gomez comes over. "Everything okay?" he asks, looking from me to my aunt.

My aunt stretches out her hand. "I'm Bennett's aunt, Laura Strausser."

Mr. Gomez introduces himself and quickly turns back

to me. "Bennett, we'll do whatever you need or want us to do right now. One of us can come back with you. Or we can let you do this *alone*." He seems to kind of emphasize that last word.

"I don't think this is the best time for Bennett to be asserting his independence," Aunt Laura says icily.

The nurse sighs loudly. "I have other patients that need my attention, so if we could just . . ."

"Yes, of course," my aunt says emphatically. "Let's get going, Bennett."

Mr. Gomez isn't about to be bullied by my aunt. "Is this okay with you, Bennett?"

I don't know what's okay with me.

But I know what isn't. Standing here in the middle of the hallway in front of a waiting room full of people while my aunt makes a scene.

"Whatever," I mumble. Mr. Gomez doesn't look convinced. But he sits back down by his wife.

"Okay, then, if you'll both follow me." The nurse hurries off in the direction of the ICU, leaving my aunt and me to keep up.

• • •

The ICU itself has a whole mess of doctors and nurses moving quickly from one small, curtained area to the next. The only things dividing the patients from one another are thick blue sheets hanging from metal tracks. Maybe the sheets don't let you see stuff, but they sure as heck still let you hear stuff. Coughing, moaning, beeping, puking, hiccuping, and gurgling. An unhappy infant screams bloody murder. What sounds like an older teenager swears behind one nearby curtain. Yeah, I'm glad for the sheets.

We hustle past some empty gurneys and young guys in blue pajamalike scrubs who are drinking coffee from Styrofoam cups. It seems as if everywhere I look there are gunmetal gray machines with cords hanging like vines in a sterilized jungle.

Finally, we stop outside another blue curtain. Checking her clipboard, the nurse makes a quick mark or two with her pencil and pulls back the curtain just a bit to peek inside. She lets it fall closed and faces me.

"Your dad's in there with Dr. Kelly now. The doctor is checking his vitals and then she'll be right out to talk to you. If you and your aunt want to stand over there,"— she points to a small, out-of-the-way spot near a water cooler—"I'm sure it won't be more than a minute or two."

And then she practically jogs off, flipping through her clipboard for her next assignment.

My aunt and I wait. I shuffle from foot to foot awkwardly. We don't talk. She glances at me now and then like she wants to say something, but I won't meet her eyes. She picks at the polish on her thumb.

Finally, a small hand pushes aside the curtain of my dad's room. A tiny woman with kind brown eyes and large, bright red glasses walks our way.

"You must be Bennett," she says, and sticks out her

hand. "I'm Dr. Kelly." My hand is clammy; but if she's grossed out, she doesn't let on. She offers my aunt a hand, too, and then smiles warmly at both of us.

"Well, I'm sure you've been pretty worried the past few hours, wondering what happened to your dad, so I'll get right to the point." She looks directly at me. "I have some good news, and I have some bad news."

CHAPTER 4
The Big Aunt Laura Takeover

"The good news, Bennett," the doctor says evenly, like she's giving me my grade on a math test, "is that your dad is very much alive; and it looks like he's going to pull through."

I feel my shoulders relax as a weight lifts from them. My dad is alive! I take a deep breath and let it out slowly. My dad is ALIVE! *Whew!*

"Thank God," my aunt breathes softly.

"But he's in pretty bad shape. That's the bad news. He's had a stroke. Basically, a blood vessel that was supplying his brain with oxygen clogged up. Without getting the stuff it needed, that part of the brain shut down, some of it permanently. We had to do surgery to repair the damage, but we won't know the extent of his injuries for a few more days. Bennett, I don't have to tell you that your dad's health isn't so great. He's extremely overweight, and the demands on his body are enormous."

A stroke.

It wasn't a heart attack then.

A stroke. Don't old people have strokes? My dad is what . . . like forty-two? How could he have a stroke?

I picture this old guy who used to live a few doors down from Grandma Jean in her nursing home. He'd had a stroke. Some days when I visited, he'd be sitting out in the front reception area. His arms would hang all kind of limplike on the edges of his wheelchair, and his head would drop just a little bit to one side. He'd smile at me in this lopsided way, as if one side of his mouth wouldn't work; and it probably didn't. One time as I passed him, he called out to me. It sounded as if someone had stuffed marshmallows in his cheeks.

"Yo shoos uh ty," he slurred, pointing a shaky finger at me. Startled and more than a little freaked out, I looked at the nurse who was taking me to see my grandma.

She smiled. "Mr. Henderson is just letting you know your shoe's untied," she explained pleasantly. "Thanks, Mr. Henderson. Always the safety monitor, aren't you?"

Is that going to be my dad from now on?

Suddenly, my lungs feel like they're being squeezed by pliers. I fight the urge to rush out the nearest exit and gulp fresh air. I try to get a grip on the truth: my dad has had a stroke. He probably has brain damage. He could be the next Mr. Henderson. I might be pushing his wheelchair around for the rest of my life . . . or his.

But he's alive. That's something, right? A big something.

"Can I see him?" I ask.

"Yes. But I've got to warn you: it's a pretty scary sight right now. Your dad's hooked up to a bunch of machines, and he's not conscious. If you were any younger, I'd say 'No way.' But I also know that seeing your dad's chest rise and fall might be just enough to put some fears to rest. If you think you can handle it, I'll let you see him." She pauses. "Bennett, I've got to ask. It doesn't say anything about your mom on my chart . . ." She lets her sentence dribble off and stares at me.

I don't know what to say. Am I not allowed to see my dad if my mom isn't here to go with me?

"Bennett lost his mom to cancer when he was five," Aunt Laura declares firmly. "I'm his aunt. I'll be taking care of him until his dad is well."

What? Whoa! Hold on a second! With my dad out of commission for a while, sure, I'll need *someplace* to go. But to Aunt Laura's? It's not like we've discussed this or anything. What gives her the right to just assume I'll stay with her?

Dr. Kelly eyes my aunt coolly. "I appreciate your willingness to help out the family. Bennett's lucky to have a relative so close." Lucky? Shyeah, right. "But with both of Bennett's parents unable to make provisions for him at the moment, unless you have a legal document somewhere that gives you guardianship, we'll need to have you speak with social services."

Aunt Laura waves her hand dismissively. "That's fine. I'll sign whatever I need to." She looks at me for a long moment. Again I refuse to meet her eyes. "I'm certain Paul didn't plan for this," she says, leaving no doubt about how disgusted she is with my father's shortsightedness. "I can assure you, however, that Bennett has no other options but to stay with me."

Dr. Kelly doesn't blink, but her lips purse.

Anger rises in my throat. Who does my aunt think she is? There's no way I'm letting her run my life . . . even temporarily.

But then my shoulders sag. Because she's right. I *don't* have a lot of choices.

No doubt the Gomezes would take me in a heartbeat. P. G. would probably let me sleep on his floor. But they have four kids, and their *abuela* already living under their roof. And their house is pretty tiny: one bathroom for all those people. It doesn't seem fair to ask them to take in one more person.

And my other family members don't offer much hope, either. My dad's sister, Aunt Molly, would probably be willing to have me stay with her in Vegas, but that means being far away from my dad. Grandma Jean has only one tiny room of her own; even if I could stay there, she'd only want me to hand over the day's newspaper or to find her stupid, dead cat.

Aunt Laura is not my favorite choice. She's simply my *only* choice. For now, anyway. My stomach tightens.

"I'll make a note to have social services give you a call

later today, then," Dr. Kelly says. "You can work this out with them. I think right now, we need to focus on Bennett and his father."

The doctor looks at me. Compassion fills her eyes.

"Bennett, it might be a good idea if your aunt went in with you. You okay with that?" Doctor Kelly stares at me.

Here's the thing: I'm really good at standing up for myself . . . in my head. When it comes to actually getting my mouth to say the words, I suck.

So even though the *last* thing I want is Aunt Laura in the room with my dad and me, my mouth blurts out, "Yeah." Aunt Laura swings open the blue curtain before I can explain that what I really mean is *Not in this lifetime!* And there we are, inside my dad's little "room."

Dr. Kelly's right. My dad looks like crap. At least three monitors blip steadily while about a dozen cords snake from him to scary-looking machines. Dad's eyes are closed. His skin is pale and saggy. But his chest is rising and falling, although weakly. I want to place my hand on it for a second, the way he'd said my mom and he did when I was a baby asleep in my crib. But my dad and I, well, we don't touch really, unless it's in a manly, "high five" kind of way. So I keep my hand by my side, curled into a tight fist.

Hospitals have this certain smell, you know? It's like antiseptic and bleach and something mediciney. I'd smelled this smell before. When I watched my mom's skin turn so pale it became see-through. When I held her hand as she tried so hard to smile, but anyone could see even that hurt. When she closed her eyes for the last time, and my family went from three to just two.

"You okay?" Aunt Laura asks.

I know what must be running through her mind: *I told you so* and *I knew this would happen*. She's always so smug and flippin' sure of herself. I can't bear to blame my dad for this and so I begin blaming her. Anger feels better than whatever this thing I'm feeling is.

I look at the man who has been my whole world for the past eight years. Watched every Dodgers game with me. Taken me fishing because I really wanted to go, even though he has a crazy fear of worms. Slept on the hard floor by my bed for a week when I had pneumonia. Found a way to pay for a Wii two Christmases ago because it was all I could talk about for months.

Am I okay? What a totally stupid question. No. I'm scared and I'm mad and I'm tired. I'm going to be moving in with an aunt I can't stand, cousins I barely know, and an uncle whose idea of fun is a relaxing five-mile jog around the neighborhood.

"Bennett, listen. We'll get you through this. We'll get your dad through this, too. But right now, I think we should get you out of here. You need some time to process all this. I promise I'll bring you back first thing in the morning, if that's what you want. But you can't do anything for your dad tonight."

She's wrong. I can curl up on the floor by his side like he would have done for me. I can turn on a Dodgers game and talk to him about baseball until he wakes up. I can promise we'll never eat fries with extra salt again.

But it's my brain saying all that. My mouth, as usual, betrays me.

"Yeah."

Hating her and hating myself even more, I let Aunt Laura lead me out of that room, away from my dad.

In the waiting room, Mr. Gomez immediately offers to let me stay with them, which my aunt dismisses with a wave and the words "Thank you, but I think Bennett needs his family right now." Mr. Gomez looks ready to argue; but Mrs. Gomez gently places a hand on his arm, and he backs off.

"Benito," she says softly, looking me in the eye. "We think of you as part of our family. You ever need us, please call. *Sí?*"

I nod, swallowing a lump in my throat.

P. G. taps his knuckles against mine. "I'll call you tonight, Benny-man."

I walk away, leaving behind the warmth of Mrs. Gomez's hugs, the familiarity of her chimichangas, and the friend who can tell you anything about me to join a family whose blood I share but whose lives I know nothing about.

CHAPTER 5

When a Dodgers Fan Meets a Giants Fan

Last year, P. G. and I had physical education together, sixth period. By that time of day, about three hundred or so boys at my school had already been in the locker room. Which meant it reeked. Bad. Like body odor and stale farts and musky deodorant and sweaty feet.

But that isn't the part of PE we hated. We hated the part right after Mr. Alvarez took roll call. He'd snap his pencil onto his clipboard and command, "Let's go, folks!"

That was the moment we hated most.

Mr. Alvarez would point up toward the basketball courts. I say "up," because to get to them you had to climb a very steep, grassy hill. He'd then puff out one military-short whistle. And like a herd of antelope startled by a pack of hungry lions, the whole class would take off running up that awful hill.

P. G. and I would *try* to jog with our classmates. Then,

out of breath and clutching our sides in agony, we'd start walking.

Mr. Alvarez would swoop up behind us and toot his whistle. "Gomez! Robinson! Pick up the pace!"

We'd bust out a few more wobbly steps, gasping, until we couldn't possibly run one more step. Then we'd settle into a walk again. By the time we reached the rest of the group, the other fifty-four kids in our class would be stretching on the blacktop. Once they'd even started playing Frisbee golf without us. It was humiliating. Or it would have been without P. G. by my side.

"You think Alvarez ever takes that whistle off, man?" P. G. would ask as we huffed along. "His poor kids. He probably whistles at them to do everything." P. G. puffed out his cheeks and deepened his voice to sound like Alvarez. "Finish that homework, men! Dishes, men, dishes!"

I'd bust out laughing, and the sense of failure and humiliation would go away.

When I first met P. G., I was a skinny little kid who never smiled and barely ever talked. My mom had just died. My dad was keeping to himself, grieving in his own way. I'd become the lowest-maintenance five-year-old ever. My house was so quiet that first year after we lost Mom, I bet the neighbors wondered if we were even home most of the time.

P. G. and I both turned up in Ms. Hunter's kindergarten

class that fall. It was late September, which in Southern California means it's blazing hot. At recess, some of the kids were running around on the soccer field, chasing a dusty, near-flat playground ball. I'd chosen to sit on the grass under a sickly looking avocado tree. I was paging through a picture book on baseball, which Ms. Hunter had let me take outside special, probably because I had a dead mom.

Suddenly, this kid ran right in front of me, kicking up dust. It was P. G., with two second graders close on his heels. One of them held up a red kick ball as if he was going to peg P. G. any minute. I watched P. G. motor around the playground, trying to dodge what was sure to be a hard throw. P. G. was losing ground rapidly.

"Come on, P. G.! We're gonna catch you sometime! We always do!" one of the boys yelled, a kid named Grayson. He was the kind of kid who deliberately pushed over your milk carton as he whipped by your table at lunch.

The other boy laughed loudly. "What's P. G. stand for, anyway?"

"Probably 'Pig Guts'!" howled Grayson, pretty sure he was the funniest guy on the playground.

P. G. stopped running and turned to face them. "Poco Gallo," he answered matter-of-factly. "'Little Rooster' in Spanish."

Even at age five I knew that was a bad move.

"Little Rooster?! LITTLE Rooster?" screamed

Grayson. "No way! Nothing's little about you, P. G."

P. G., clueless or brave, I wasn't sure which, explained calmly, "I'm always the first one awake in the morning. Like a rooster."

"Let's see if you can squawk like a rooster," Grayson said, and raised his arm to fire.

P. G. ducked behind the slide just in time, and the chase was on again.

It didn't take long for the shot to find its mark, though. After the ball crashed into his gut, P. G. went down like a wounded soldier and curled up into a ball.

The boys stood over him for a few seconds, laughing and giving him a few nudges with their feet. Then they ran off to find another victim.

Eventually, P. G. rolled over, sat up, and brushed himself off, and began wandering around the playground again.

I did something then that I hadn't done for a while: I spoke.

"Hey!" I called out softly. "Want to look at some baseball pictures?"

P. G. gave me a "whatever" shrug. I would figure out later that very little ruffled P. G. Not playground balls fired like missiles. Not teachers who made you run a mile. Not girls who were too pretty to ever like an overweight, unpopular kid.

He plopped down next to me. "Who's your team?" he

asked, glancing at the open page, which happened to be about Sandy Koufax, the best left-handed pitcher of all time.

"Dodgers. Who's yours?" I asked.

P. G. grinned and wiggled his eyebrows up and down a few times. "Giants."

"No way. Seriously?" I said.

And that's when our friendship was cemented.

Thank God, eight years later, I still had P. G.

CHAPTER 6
Deflated

Later that night, after a quick trip to my house to grab some of my stuff, social services calls. We'd talked to them for a minute or two before leaving the hospital, but I guess they need more information or something.

"The woman will be here tomorrow with some papers to sign," my aunt tells my uncle after the call. "Since no one has any clue if Paul established guardianship, they need to make sure you and I are capable of the job." She crosses her arms and perches on the arm of the couch. "I don't know why this has to be such a hassle. It's not like Bennett has anywhere else to go."

My uncle Jim shooshes her with a sidelong glance at me. I pretend to be engrossed in the Animal Planet show that my cousin Josh is watching. I'm too numb and too tired to really care, anyway.

• • •

I'm sitting with Dad, munching on vending machine food. Since I've gotten to Aunt Laura's, I've craved Ding Dongs or Doritos or something with a reasonable amount of *taste* so badly I've been getting the shakes just thinking about them. I curse my fate for the ninetieth time in two days and look at Dad. He's still hooked up to about a dozen machines, all of which are monitoring different things on his body. His eyes are closed. I could trace his bluish veins through his see-through skin if I wasn't scared to touch him.

I decide to call P. G. from my cell phone.

"How is he, man?" he asks.

"The same." I'm trying to keep the despair from my voice. "The doctors tell me to wait, this is normal, the brain takes time to heal—all that stuff."

"Sucks, dude."

"What if he doesn't wake up, P. G.?" It's the first time I've asked that question out loud, though I've thought it about a hundred times.

"Don't go there, man," P. G. says quickly. "Think positive, right? You got to hope for the best."

We talk for a few more minutes, trying to focus on stuff like baseball and video games and some cute girl P. G. met at the mall; but it's a struggle for me. When I click my phone shut, the reality of what's happened to my family sets in. I walk over to Dad and look down, wanting to shake him awake.

I feel so utterly alone. And, yeah, a little bit pissed that he's left me like this.

But mostly, I'm just deflated, like a tire who's met a nail.

Hesitantly, I reach out my hand.

His hand is cold but soft. I realize I haven't touched my dad, not like this, in a long time. Thirteen-year-old guys don't really touch their dads much, I guess. Do they? But as I touch him now, I know that this no-touching thing is a stupid rule. If he wakes up—no, *when* he wakes up—I'll touch my dad more. Hug him. Heck, I might even kiss his cheek now and then. He deserves that from me; but more than that, it just feels right.

I brush my hands together and wipe the Doritos crumbs on my jeans. Then I gently grab his hand and squeeze.

"Dad. Look, I know you and me have some changes to make. Eat right. Exercise. That whole thing. But if it means you're going to be around for a while longer, then it's good with me. Okay?"

I kneel by his bedside, clutching his hand.

"Come on, Dad. For real. I need you."

I didn't feel the tears start, but here they are.

"Wake up, Dad. Speak. Walk. Root for the stupid Dodgers. We'll start eating right, and we'll work out or whatever it is we have to do."

I stay kneeling for a second, my forehead resting on the edge of my dad's bed. I suddenly feel pretty drained. My knees start to ache. Slowly, I haul myself back up to my feet and return to my chair.

A nurse comes in, throws me a wave, and runs through her checklist of tests. The doctor comes in and grunts over my dad's chart. My aunt Molly leaves a message on my cell wanting to know how Dad's doing. And P. G. texts me scores for both the Giants and the Dodgers.

Dad doesn't move. Not a single twitch.

CHAPTER 7
Operation: Get Bennett Healthy

I spend most of the next four days in that stuffy, sick-smelling room with my dad. I become well-acquainted with the vending machines, the nurses, and the television set—which, by the way, only has basic cable so you can't watch jack. I read every magazine from the volunteer: a cute high school freshman who hands them to me with pity-filled eyes but makes sure not to touch my hand in the exchange.

And I eat. A lot. Mostly junk. Oreo cookies and Ding Dongs and potato chips and hot dogs from the cafeteria. With each bite I'm conscious that this is exactly what got my dad into this hospital bed. But each bite helps soothe the gnawing ache in my belly.

On Thursday afternoon, my aunt picks me up from the hospital after another four hours of me talking to what feels like an empty room.

"Ten minutes until dinner," she says when we walk in the door. "Josh is cooking again."

There's some good news, at least.

I trudge upstairs to my new room: the "lighthouse" room. Every room in Aunt Laura's house has a theme: the "garden" room (aka the den), the "soccer" room (Kiley's), the "ducklings" room (the bathroom), the "country picnic" room (the kitchen). Walls are neatly painted, and each room has some kind of matching wallpaper border running around the top of it. Fancy little pillows are on every couch and chair. Sometimes it feels as if I'm living in one of those houses you see on the home-decorating channels.

My uncle sticks his head in my room a few moments later. He just got home from Kiley's soccer practice.

"How's your dad, sport?"

"Uh, the same, I guess."

He shakes his head and sighs. "Hang in there, kid." He disappears.

Uncle Jim is a tall, athletic man who has called me "sport" ever since I can remember. Don't get me wrong; he seems like a nice-enough guy. But just being around him makes you feel like you need to swig Gatorade and stretch out your hamstrings or something. He begins each day with a run at dawn, trots off to his job at a sports therapy clinic, bounds in the door for dinner, and then hurries out the door again to coach one of his many teams.

Kiley is about six months younger than me. I've pretty much decided that thirteen-year-old girls, in general, are not an easy bunch to like. They seem to flip their hair a lot and curl their top lips as if I'm the most disgusting creature they've ever seen. Given the way Kiley and all her beanpole friends look, I probably am.

Josh is a different story. I really like Josh. He's two years younger than me, a pip-squeak of a kid with curly brown hair that clings tightly to his head. Josh's favorite thing to do is cook. And, man, can that boy cook.

Monday night was the first night I got to see Josh in action. While he chopped onions, Josh explained to me that he liked to choose healthy recipes but make them taste good. He understands instinctively how to season food and what tastes go together. Someday Josh is going to open his own restaurant. I plan to have a standing reservation.

The other thing I like about Josh, besides his grilled garlic-and-lime chicken, is that he listens. *Really* listens. He cocks his head and rests his chin on his hands and looks at me as if what I'm saying is the most important thing in the world. If I say something funny, he'll get this slow-spreading grin, and his eyes will crinkle up. And although he doesn't say much in return, I get the feeling that he remembers every word I say.

After I throw on a clean T-shirt, I head downstairs to find Josh.

"Hey, Bennett." He offers an easy smile. He's rubbing a roast with some spicy mixture he's no doubt concocted himself.

We chat about his day and some new video game he

wants to get. Josh pops his roast in the oven, sets the timer, and begins chopping vegetables for a salad.

"How's soccer going?" I ask him, reaching for one of the carrot pieces he's just cut. I don't know much about soccer, but I know Josh had practice earlier that day and that Uncle Jim is his coach. I make a mental note to find out his game schedule so I can go see him play.

Josh whacks at the carrot a few more times before he answers.

"Sometimes, I wish . . ." His voice tapers off. I wait, looking at him as he starts neatly chopping some radishes. "I'm not very good at sports. I don't even really like them, you know?"

"So why do you play them then?"

"Because . . ." Josh sighs, but won't look at me. "Because it makes my dad so happy. It's all he's ever wanted. A son he could coach. But, really, Kiley's a whole lot better at soccer than me. And she likes it, too."

I want to say, *Just tell your dad how you feel.* But that would be kind of hypocritical. Do I ever speak up and say how I'm feeling? Shyeah, right. I decide to listen, like Josh.

Josh stops chopping for a minute and meets my gaze. "I'm glad you're here."

"Well, thanks." I'm not sure what else to say.

"I mean, I'm not glad your dad is in the hospital. But it's nice having another guy around the house. Kind of like having an older brother."

He starts back in on the radishes, and I don't say anything. A few minutes later I slip quietly out of the room. As I climb my way back to my room, I realize that the knots in my stomach have loosened. Just a little.

• • •

Friday morning at breakfast Josh offers to come to the hospital with me for an hour or two. Aunt Laura is going to drop us off, run a few errands, and pick us up around lunchtime so Josh can make it to his afternoon cooking class. Since my dad's stroke, I've been spending the whole day at the hospital, and my aunt or uncle has picked me up each day before dinner.

"I'd like to stay at the hospital this afternoon," I announce boldly, studying my plate and fork with intensity. The idea of spending the afternoon with HER is not appealing.

Aunt Laura's making whole wheat, low-fat pancakes. I suspect this is part of Operation: Get Bennett Healthy. Little does she know I'm still sneaking Hostess CupCakes at the hospital.

With her spatula poised to flip another pancake, she turns to me suddenly.

"Um, well, I wanted to talk to you about that." My stomach flips along with the pancake. "Today is registration at Truman Middle School."

I feel the knots in my stomach retighten. Of course, registration day: when we pick up our class schedules, buy our PE clothes, and take our pictures for the yearbook.

51

I'd totally forgotten. Would they still let me register at Truman now that I'm living in a different school district with my aunt?

"How do you feel about continuing at Truman?" Aunt Laura asks.

She drops a pancake on my plate. I stare at it doubtfully. Maybe with enough syrup . . .

"Uh, fine." Kiley and Josh go to Meadowbrook Middle School, which isn't too far from here. Transferring to Meadowbrook hasn't even been on my radar screen. Of course I would keep going to the school by my house, right?

"Good. Your uncle and I talked about it, and we think you should go to Truman instead of transferring to Meadowbrook this fall."

Josh's head jerks up from his pancakes with interest. Kiley looks like she's biting back a smile. I can almost feel the waves of relief wafting off of her.

"Uh, okay," I say stupidly, even though I'm pretty irritated. I mean, I'm really glad that I'll be going to my same old school, but what gives her the right to make decisions for me as if she's my parent? I stab my syrup-drenched pancake and shove the whole lumpy mess into my mouth angrily. My aunt grimaces. I ignore her.

"We'll all have to get up earlier in order to drive you over there, drop you off, and make it back before Kiley and Josh's school starts; but I think it'll be easier for you in the long run." She clears my plate while she talks.

Good thing I don't want seconds, I guess, huh?

I sit there. Silent. Fuming. If I were a cartoon character, I'm sure steam would have been coming out of my ears. I shove out of my chair, its legs scraping the floor loudly, and stomp out of the room. And believe me, when a two-hundred and fifty-pound kid stomps, you can feel it.

• • •

Josh and I walk in silence to my dad's hospital room. I gently push open the door. The curtains are all drawn. It has that same sick smell as before, though it isn't as strong. Or I've gotten used to it.

My dad has a new doctor now, a tall, Middle Eastern guy named Dr. Abari. I don't think he likes me much for some reason, or maybe he just doesn't like kids. Or maybe he doesn't like anyone.

No nurses or doctors are checking vitals or refilling drip bags at the moment, so Josh and I make ourselves at home. I slide back all the curtains to let in some California sunshine. Josh flips on the TV, while I push a button on my dad's remote to raise his head a little bit.

All of this is lost on my dad. He hasn't opened his eyes in seven days.

"Hey, Dad." I glance over him as I straighten his blanket. The doctor has told me to talk to him as much as possible. There's a chance he can hear me and come out of his coma if he recognizes a familiar voice. Those first few days it felt weird, talking to someone who didn't . . . or couldn't . . . talk back. But I'm getting used to it now.

"Dodgers games tonight and tomorrow. Padres, man. I'll let you know the score when I come tomorrow. Should be a good series," I add. "Oh, and hey, Josh is here today. We're going to play some cards for a bit and then I have to leave early. I've got to register for school this afternoon."

At the table in the corner of the room, Josh is pulling out a deck of cards and shuffling them. I sit down across from him, and he starts to deal.

"Hey, Bennett," he says. "Why were you so mad this morning? Did you *want* to go to my school?"

I pick up my cards and begin organizing them. Just thinking about the conversation makes me angry all over again.

"No, not really. But I was angry because your mom decided what school I was going to and she's not, like, *my* mom, you know? I don't want to go to Meadowbrook. I mean, P. G. goes to Truman; and, anyway, my dad's probably going to be back to normal in a few weeks, and then I'd have to transfer back."

"Yeah." Josh nods. "That's mom. She tries to keep everybody all, like, organized and on track. It can be a pain." He throws down a card. Dang. Nine of hearts. I need the nine of spades for gin. "You really think you'll be back home in a few weeks?"

"I don't know." I shrug. "I really hope so." I pick up a card from the pile. Discard it.

Josh keeps his eyes on his cards and doesn't respond.

"Hey," I say casually. "Even when I move back home,

we can still hang out, you know? I kind of like having a younger cousin around to pick on."

He half chuckles. He grabs my discarded card. "Yeah. Me, too."

I'm one card away from hollering "Gin!" when I catch a movement out of the corner of my eye. Josh does, too, because his head swivels in the direction of my dad. I lay down my cards and stand up.

Dad looks just the same. Peaceful, pale, a little thin in the face since his diet has gone from cheeseburgers to whatever yellow fluid is being fed into his stomach. I'm about to sit down and resume the game when I swear I see my dad's left hand twitch.

"Josh!" I whisper. "Did you see that?" I push back my chair. I'm ready to holler for a nurse, but I want to make sure I'm not imagining it.

"I did, Bennett." Josh's eyes are wide, sincere. "His hand moved."

"Dad?" I take a step toward him. "Dad? Can you hear me? It's Bennett, Dad. Open your eyes if you can hear me."

For a few seconds—but it seems way longer than that—I wait. I don't breathe. But nothing happens. I stare hard at his left hand. It remains completely motionless.

"It moved, Bennett," Josh says quietly. "I swear it did."

"Yeah. I thought so, too." I search my dad's closed-up face. "Dad, please open your eyes."

And he does.

CHAPTER 8
Hope

Once the nurses get wind that my dad opened his eyes, things happen really quickly. A lot of call buttons are pushed, and Dr. Abari is there before I can start yelling his name. Josh and I stay off to the side, out of the way but close enough that I can still see my dad's face.

It isn't long, though, before they shoosh us out of the room. This seems stupid to me, because if I'd just woken up out of a week-long coma, I'd want to see my son, not some strange doctor who doesn't smile . . . ever. I step outside reluctantly.

I text P. G. and tell him what's going on. He writes simply, "TG." Yeah, thank God.

After about ten minutes I'm ready to pull the fire alarm handle if it means clearing out the room so I can see my dad. My stomach feels the way it does when I have to give an oral report in front of the class. Josh doesn't speak, which is good, because I'd probably bite his head off. He seems to know this instinctively and keeps his mouth shut.

Two more minutes pass—I'm watching the time on my cell phone with growing annoyance—when suddenly the door opens and everyone files out. I find myself face-to-face with Dr. Abari, who looks pretty serious. But then again, he always looks pretty serious.

"Come on in, Bennett," he says, holding open the door as if we're stepping into a fancy restaurant instead of my dad's hospital room.

Dad's eyes are closed. Once again he lays motionless.

I whirl around to Dr. Abari. "He opened his eyes! I swear it! Ask Josh. He saw it! Tell him, Josh!"

Josh is nodding his head like his life depends on it, but the doctor holds up his hand.

"Hold on, Bennett," he says. "I know he opened his eyes. I saw him, too. And the good news is that his pupils reacted to the light I shone in them. That's fantastic news. He squeezed my hand when I asked him to, which is even better news. But that few minutes of interaction probably wiped him out. Don't worry, though, Bennett. We're close now. We'll get him back."

"I wanted him to see me." I hear the whine in my voice and grimace. "Why did I have to leave?"

"I'm sorry, Bennett," Dr. Abari says, showing his first trace of true sincerity. "Sometimes when stroke victims open their eyes suddenly, it can indicate something new going on in their brain—and that something is not always good. We had to make sure he wasn't suffering an additional stroke. But we don't think that was the case.

Keep talking to him. Keep squeezing his hand. Let him know you're here. But don't be alarmed if he doesn't move any more today. This is a positive sign, Bennett. This is fantastic news, really. We have hope that he'll be on his road to recovery quickly."

That word catches me.

Hope.

It hangs in the room long after the doctor leaves. Josh goes off to call his mom, and it's just me and my dad. Somehow I can still feel that word reverberating off the walls of the room, finding its way to my dad and me, settling in around our shoulders like a warm blanket.

Hope. It feels good. I reach out and hold my dad's hand. Firmly, like a son should.

CHAPTER 9
Control Freak

Somehow I talk Aunt Laura into letting me stay the rest of the afternoon with my dad at the hospital. Josh convinces her that he can pick up my class schedule from Truman without me. I settle in a chair and wait for my dad to wake up again.

He doesn't.

He lays frustratingly still. But now that I know he *might* wake up at any second, I don't plan to leave this room until my dad opens his eyes and sees me. Later, after a lot of pleading, I even talk the nurses—and my aunt—into letting me sleep on a cot next to his bed that night. My way of paying Dad back for all those pneumonia nights.

The next morning, one of my favorite nurses, Gretta, brings me a yummy chocolate doughnut and some orange juice. Then, promising to return later, she leaves me alone with my dad.

I scrutinize every inch of him. Has he moved? Are

his hands in exactly the same place as last night? Is his expression the same? Did he open his eyes while I was sleeping and then fade out again because I didn't respond?

Uncle Jim, Aunt Laura, Kiley, and Josh get to the hospital around nine thirty. I'm almost nodding off again when they come in.

"Rise and shine, sport!" my uncle booms.

I think I jump nearly high enough to hit my head on the ceiling.

Josh smiles with his whole face.

"How's your dad?" my aunt asks, coming over to his bed. She looks down at him but keeps her arms folded across her chest. "Has he opened his eyes again?"

"No." Why can't they just go away?

"Sorry, Bennett," Josh says with all the sincerity in the world. My heart feels like a brick.

Kiley, who's dressed in black nylon shorts and her bright yellow soccer jersey, hasn't taken more than one step into the room. "*Mom*," she whines, drawing out that one-syllable word for at least three seconds. "My game? Remember?"

And with that, my aunt launches into plan mode.

"Kiley's game starts in about an hour, and we thought we could all go and support her. Then we'll grab some lunch and bring you back here for an hour or two. We're going out tonight with some friends, and Kiley has plans, too. So you'll hang out with Josh at home."

Dang. Is there anything she isn't going to take over in my life? My hairstyle? My friends?

It isn't that I mind doing any of it. In fact, she's been carting me around, so I probably owe her some free babysitting. But why can't she just *ask*? My dad would've asked me.

Without waiting for my response, Aunt Laura looks down again at the motionless man in the bed. I think she's so used to running her life according to a schedule that she sometimes forgets to stop and really *care* for a second. If you can't cross it off a list, then it doesn't really matter to Aunt Laura.

What I wouldn't give to see my dad sit up right now and calmly say, "Laura, I think my son and I will be going home now. Thanks for all your help this week. So long."

But he doesn't sit up. He stays unmoving as my aunt, uncle, and cousins file out of the room.

I trail along behind them, trying to communicate my annoyance through my slumped shoulders and scowling face. I avoid Josh's hopeful eyes but cast just one glance back at my dad, hoping for a miracle that doesn't come.

CHAPTER 10
Aunt Laura, One. Bennett, Zero.

The next afternoon my dad opens his eyes again and even tries to speak.

"Guh . . . mmmm . . . uhgh . . . grrrr." After a lot of trial and error, I figure out that this means "Bring me a glass of water."

Yeah, it's going to be a long road to recovery for both Dad *and* me.

Still, Dr. Abari assures me that this is a positive sign. "Your dad is going to need literally months of retraining his mouth and brain to work together. But within a week or so you should start to see some progress, and he'll probably be able to say some simple words."

There are moments where I can see the frustration and confusion in my dad's eyes. I get a yucky feeling in my stomach thinking about him being unable to tell me what he wants, what he's feeling, what he's been through.

But in the next moment I'll just feel relief and happiness. My dad is alive and awake. I'm not going to lose him.

I munch on Snickers and Twinkies and talk to him until his eyes close again.

"Another hot one today, Dad," I say, closing the blinds to the sun when I feel armpit sweat coming on. "Dodgers game tonight. Away. Against the Mets. We should take 'em easily."

As I babble on, I note every small movement of his hands and every miraculous blink of his eyes. This time when he closes his eyes again, I don't feel that hole in my stomach. I know he'll wake up again.

• • •

That evening I hang out with Josh, and I'm so happy, I play every video and board game he wants. He could've suggested dressing up like Ken and Barbie, and I would have done it with a smile on my face. I feel that good.

Kiley gets home about ten.

She glances up from her phone long enough to nod in my direction. "How's your dad, Bennett?"

"Seems better today," I say.

Her thumbs are already flying across her keypad. "Cool," she says, and hops up the stairs to go to bed, or do whatever teenage girls do.

Josh starts snoring halfway into the third *Pirates of the Caribbean* movie, sprawled across one couch. I'm slouched in the other, too amped up to sleep, wondering if I would look as good as Johnny Depp with an earring.

I hear the lock click in the door at about 11 p.m. but don't make a move to get up.

"Hey, Bennett!" Uncle Jim says, bounding in the door as if it's morning and he can't wait to get his day started. The man's never tired. It must be those sport drinks he guzzles.

"Bennett, good, you're still awake." Aunt Laura, quick and businesslike, removes her heeled shoes and neatly places them on the bottom step of the staircase. She stops to tenderly brush aside a lock of Josh's hair before sitting rigidly in a chair across from me.

"Laura," Uncle Jim says cautiously. "Are you sure you want to do this tonight? We're all tired and . . ."

"We might not have time tomorrow with church and all. Better to discuss it now."

Uncle Jim sighs, but doesn't object. I wonder what big discussion can't wait until the morning. This can't be good. My fragile balloon of happiness floats dangerously close by.

"Your uncle and I were talking tonight, Bennett." My aunt speaks cautiously, as if I might throw a tantrum any minute.

"I won't beat around the bush. We're worried about your health. Your eating habits aren't the best, and we've yet to see you do much physical activity. I've noticed you're often out of breath by the time you reach the top of the stairs. With what your father has gone through, well, we're afraid of what might happen to you if you don't make some changes. And, frankly, we'd like to help."

My happy balloon starts to lose air. Fast.

She'd like to *help*? Control my life is more like it. I rage at her inside my head. *What do you know about my eating habits? I've been eating your flippin' broccoli since I've gotten here, haven't I?* I start to stand up. I don't need to hear this crap.

But I've sunk so far into the couch that it takes a heck of a lot of effort to push my body up and out of the cushions. Using my elbows, I manage to scoot my butt to the edge. I lean forward.

"See, the thing is—" I start in a low, controlled voice.

"Your uncle and I . . . ," Aunt Laura interrupts, stopping to clear her throat. She shoots an annoyed glance at Uncle Jim, who is fiddling with his watch and not saying a word.

"Here is what we'd like to see. Starting tomorrow, your uncle is going to take you on his morning jogs. We don't expect you to be able to keep up with him at first. But we thought it would be a great way for you to get into better shape while you're with us."

Pop! Pop! Pop! My happy balloon is toast.

I won't look at her. A morning *jog* with ultraenergized Uncle Jim? *That* should be fun. Watch how the teenager can't keep up with his forty-year-old uncle! See Bennett gasp and pant!

Aunt Laura must have been shooting Uncle Jim nasty looks, because suddenly he clears his throat. "Listen,

Bennett. You're dealing with a lot of changes right now, and we hate to throw one more at you."

"But you will, anyway."

Silence. I still won't look at them.

Finally my uncle clears his throat again and continues. "Your aunt and I were just kind of hoping that maybe we could teach you how to live healthier. So when your dad comes home and it's the two of you, you'll be able to help him and prevent this from happening again." He exhales long and hard.

"We've laid out a workout plan for you; and starting tomorrow, you'll be on a low-calorie, low-fat diet," my aunt chimes in.

I have to give it to them. It's beautifully played. They pulled the dad card and everything. Help yourself and help your dad, too, right? And, by the way, we've got everything all planned out. Just sign here on the dotted line.

I'm pissed.

The silence is deep enough that we can hear the grandfather clock in the entryway ticking off the seconds. My aunt shifts uncomfortably on the couch and is about to speak when I cut her off. I'm literally shaking.

"I'm not a runner," I say. "I'll walk. But I won't run." I take a deep breath and force myself to continue. "And I'm not doing this because you want me to. I'm doing it for my dad." I realize I've been clenching my fists at my sides and force myself to relax them.

"Okay, then." Aunt Laura slaps her palms on her thighs. "You need to be ready by six thirty tomorrow morning. I'll have a water bottle for you to take and breakfast for you when you get back."

That settled, she rises, picks up her shoes, and walks up the stairs.

Game over. Aunt Laura, one. Bennett, zero.

As I flip off the TV and throw my blanket over Josh, I notice my uncle's still in the room. He's watching me carefully.

"I'm actually looking forward to spending some time with you, Bennett. Doing an activity I really enjoy. You might find you enjoy it, too."

I set the remote in the little basket on the table where Laura likes it to go and finally look up at him.

"Then why couldn't someone have just asked me? Why couldn't you say, 'Hey, Bennett, want to walk with me in the morning?'"

"You've got a point, Bennett. I'll talk with your aunt. . . ."

"And let me ask you this, Uncle Jim. Would you enjoy running if you were as fat as me?" I look down at my belly. "Especially when you'd gotten used to kids at school making fun of you pretty much *every* day in PE? Would you enjoy running so much then?"

I don't wait for him to respond. I just start huffing my way up the stairs to bed. Pissed that I'm huffing. Pissed that my aunt knew I would be.

• • •

In the morning I'm not good company. I sulk the whole mile Uncle Jim and I walk together. He tries to keep the mood light by pointing out stuff on our route. He's lived in this town his whole life and knows practically everyone, so he has little facts about every house on the block. I don't say a word. We walk the last quarter mile in silence, listening to my heavy breathing.

"Well, Bennett," Uncle Jim says when we reach his driveway. He's slipping ear buds into his ears for his own run. "I'm glad you came with me this morning. Same time tomorrow?"

I shrug and head up the driveway.

But secretly? The walk wasn't that bad. Uncle Jim is really too nice a guy to hate. Of course, my aunt doesn't have to know that. No way am I going to tell her.

CHAPTER 11
Fat Boy

It's the first day of school. Twelve days since my dad's stroke and six days after he opened his eyes. Today also happens to be the day my dad is leaving the hospital and moving into a new rehabilitation facility. He'll live there until he's able to function on his own again. Which—given my aunt's determination to completely take over my life—I'm really hoping is soon.

P. G. meets me on the hill behind campus. We quickly compare schedules. Turns out we only have second-period science and lunch together. Not PE. I feel my body slump. Great.

"I'm gonna have to run alone?" P. G. says. His eyes droop, and he pulls his shoulders way forward, pretending deep sadness.

"I'm sure you can find some cute girl to keep you company in the back of the pack," I tease. "You're always telling me how you've got a way with the ladies."

"That's right." P. G. nods and struts, his large belly jiggling comically. "I've got a way, man. Don't you forget it."

We both laugh and head down the hill to scope out a spot to meet for lunch and then find our first classes.

In third-period English I roam around the room, trying to find my name on one of the posted signs at each table. As I'm setting my bag on the floor, the chair next to me scrapes backward. I look up to see the most gorgeous green eyes ever.

Great. It's Taylor—the girl I've liked since last year. To my huge surprise, she smiles at me.

"Hey, Bennett." She sits down. My heart nearly stops.

"Hi, Taylor," I choke out, struggling to keep my voice even. "Did you have a good summer?"

"Yeah, it was okay. How about you?"

Well, mine sucked, actually. But I say, "Me, too. Just okay."

That's it. Nothing earth shattering. She doesn't giggle or flirt or tell me I'm everything she's ever wanted in a guy. But it's enough to keep me feeling pretty good until lunchtime. Then it's a fast trip downhill. *Way* downhill.

There's a low concrete wall that separates the lunch courtyard from the hill that leads up to the basketball courts. To everyone at Truman—even the teachers—it's known as the eighth-grade wall. Many years ago, eighth graders claimed this wall as their own, and it stuck. It's a time-honored tradition to stake out your spot that first day of school. P. G. and I picked out our spot this morning as soon as we walked down the hill. We planned to hustle here after fourth period and grab it early.

P. G. is sitting right at the spot, this little area under a palm tree. His lunch is already out on his lap. Not surprisingly, Mrs. Gomez makes mouthwatering lunches. Knowing Aunt Laura, I probably got three carrot sticks and a dry rice cake.

"Hey, P. G.!" I call when I get close. "You got it!"

"Did you doubt me, man? I told you I would get this spot, and I got it."

I plop down next to him, noting that to our right is a group of girls most would call "nerdy." I, however, having been labeled "fat" for many years, choose to call them "academically blessed," which P. G. shortened to "A.B." This really works since those are the grades they always get.

On the other side of us is a group of guys who are more hard-core. They aren't gangbangers, but they're close. Fortunately, they're in trouble a lot—suspended or at lunch detention—and they cut school pretty frequently, so chances are good that within a week their numbers will dwindle.

But we have to get through today.

Things start off just fine. P. G. and I chat about our classes. No one has commented on my dad all day, so they either don't know or don't care. I tell P. G. about Taylor. Apparently, Miranda, the girl he's had a crush on since fourth grade, said she liked his hair—a good sign in his eyes that she's hot for him.

"Look," one kid to our left says loudly. "We get to sit by the Fat Boys. You know what that means, right?"

I try not to look; but out of the corner of my eyes, I see a short, skinny kid in baggy jeans that are barely hanging on to his hips. He's got slicked-back black hair and a sneer on his face that looks as if it might be permanent.

His friends laugh.

P. G. and I pretend we haven't heard. But we quickly start grabbing our stuff.

"Means we'll have some tasty lunches, right, Fat Boys?" the kid says, coming closer.

He grabs my lunch bag from my hand. "What'd you get today, Fat Boy: chocolate cake? Cookies? Doughnuts? Come on, man, don't hold out on me."

"Sorry, man," I say, trying to sound confident. My insides have turned to jelly. "Finished everything already. Kids like me eat pretty quick, you know."

If I can laugh at myself, then laughing *at* me won't be nearly as fun for him, right?

"Ah, *gordo* thinks he's funny, guys. Is he funny, homeys?"

A really scrawny kid next to him smirks. "He ain't funny, Luis."

Luis gets in my face. "I tell you what, Fat Boy; you save me a piece of cake tomorrow, and we'll be good. Got it?"

"Sure, man, whatever." I grab my backpack and follow P. G., who's already climbing the hill.

"Go work off those calories, boys!" yells Luis. His friends cackle.

P. G. and I have been through stuff like this before. It's never fun. But P. G. doesn't let it bother him, and I try to follow his lead.

As we get to the top of the hill, breathless, P. G. mutters, "Jerks." And we drop it.

• • •

After history fifth period I trudge slowly to PE, dreading what's coming: stares as I change in the locker room from kids who seem fascinated by my mound of pale flesh, whispers when I come in last on the warm-up run, moans when I end up on anybody's team.

We're all assigned a number painted on the blacktop that we are supposed to sit on for roll call. I lower myself slowly to the ground. My legs are way too big to even think about crossing them, so I sit with them awkwardly out in front of me. I'm relieved to see there's one other really heavy kid in the class, a guy I know a little bit. His name is Drew, I think. He wanders over, plops down by me, and nods toward the kids shooting basketballs. "So, this is gonna suck pretty good, huh?"

I laugh. "Yep. PE always does. I can pull As in everything else and then I'll get a B in this stupid class. And that's after working my butt off, too."

"I hear you, bro."

Just then something small and hard hits the back of my head. I put my hand up and pull a wet, white spitball from my hair.

"Hey, *gordo!*" a voice calls from behind me. I don't have to turn around to know who it is.

"I like my chocolate cake with lots of frosting," Luis says.

"Just ignore him," Drew says under his breath. And then he calls Luis a name I won't repeat, but it fits.

Luis and his gang walk by slowly, enjoying their power. "Tomorrow, Fat Boy."

It's going to be a long year. Really long.

CHAPTER 12
Shrink

After school, P. G. is waiting for me at the top of the hill behind campus.

"*Hola*, Benito," he says cheerfully.

I'm too tired from my climb and the day to answer with any enthusiasm. I'm facing an hour's worth of homework and a half hour wait for my aunt, and I still need to find time to go see my dad.

P. G. eyes me. "What's got you in such a mood?"

Without answering, I head toward a shady grassy area and toss down my heavy backpack.

September in Southern California usually means some of the hottest temperatures of the year. Today we're nearing triple digits. Sweat is staining the armpits of my T-shirt, making a nice little crescent around my neck and dribbling in little rivers down my back. But no belly button stain—yet.

I tell him about sixth period and Luis. He shrugs.

"Shake it off, man. He's just trying to get under your skin."

"Yeah." I push Luis from my thoughts. "How was your day?"

"Ah, you know." He flops onto the grass. "Chicks throwing themselves at me, teachers blown away by my superior intelligence, the usual."

I laugh and drop down next to him.

"How's your dad, Benny-man?" His tone is low. Serious.

"Seems to be getting a little better." I wipe some sweat out of my eyes. "I'm going to see him later at this new rehab place."

I'm only allowed to visit him from nine to ten in the morning or four to five at night. Since school makes the mornings impossible, I have just that one hour every day. With homework and stuff, it probably wouldn't be possible to stay longer, anyway; but it still sucks that somebody can tell me how long I can spend with my dad.

A curt *beep!* makes us both turn our heads toward the street. Aunt Laura sits drumming her fingers on the steering wheel. I heave my backpack onto my back and struggle awkwardly to my feet.

If it had been my dad picking me up, he would have insisted on giving P. G. a ride home, too. Triple-digit temps or pouring rain, I have a pretty good feeling my aunt will never make the same offer.

Once I'm home, I have about half an hour to wolf down

some low-fat graham crackers, carrot sticks, and milk. I'm just starting my math when Uncle Jim shows up to take me to see Dad.

"So, sport," Uncle Jim says once we're in the car with the air-conditioning full blast. "How was the first day of school?"

"Okay, I guess."

"How'd PE go?"

"Pretty much like I thought."

Uncle Jim nods sympathetically.

"You know, Bennett," he says, "when I was in middle school, I wore these really thick glasses. I was a scrawny little kid, at least a foot shorter than everybody else. Basketball was a nightmare for me since even the average-sized girl could block just about any shot I made. But I was fast. I learned to run hard to make up for what I lacked in height. Then when I was about a junior in high school, I shot up. Grew about two feet. Got contacts. Suddenly I wasn't the little kid everybody could pick on anymore."

"Yeah," I say. "But I don't have a height problem. I have a size problem. Growing isn't an issue. I need to shrink."

"Then shrink," he says, like it's as easy as erasing a misspelled word in an essay. "I'm all about feeling comfortable in your own skin. But if you don't feel good about being overweight, then change it. It's not as if you're a paraplegic or have a deformity that you can't do anything about. You have the power to change this."

The car grows quiet. Uncle Jim subtly turns up the radio.

Ever since I started outweighing my classmates, I've been a target. The butt of jokes. Like the waitress who raises her eyebrows when my dad and I go into a restaurant and order two full meals, plus an appetizer and then two desserts. We took a field trip on a bus last year for school, and P. G. and I each needed our own seats because we couldn't fit together. Buying clothes is a nightmare; I often go into the men's department to find sizes that fit, but the styles aren't always the same as what kids my age are wearing.

If I'm being honest, though? Sure, I've wished to be thinner or smaller. But I've never really thought about what I need to do to change. Maybe because my dad and best friend are overweight, too, and don't make it an issue. Maybe because, deep down, I just don't think I can do it.

Uncle Jim makes it sound so simple. *Shrink*. As if I could wave my magic wand and be fifty pounds lighter.

But what if he's right? What if it isn't really all that hard?

I've been doing the morning walks for a few days, and they're not that bad. Two miles is about max for me, though. I have to get up at six thirty, walk for half an hour, and be ready to leave for school by seven thirty. But if it means kids like Luis will someday leave me alone, maybe it's a small price to pay.

"You think it's that easy?" I ask Uncle Jim as he pulls into the parking lot of the rehabilitation center. I get ready to hop out. "For me to shrink, I mean."

"Bennett." He looks at me straight on. "I'll tell you what I see. I see a kid who is likable, loyal, and very bright. Who has handled a crappy situation more calmly than most adults I know. He needs to learn to stand up for himself a little more—but then, I could probably use a lesson in that, too."

I know we're both thinking the same thing: it isn't easy to stand up to Aunt Laura.

"This kid also needs to figure out what he really wants out of life. But mostly, he needs to take a good look in a mirror and realize that underneath all that—yes, I'll say it—*fat* is a kid who can succeed. Now get out before the car behind me starts honking!"

Whoa. Nobody's ever said something like that to me before. I don't know what to do with it. But one word gets kind of stuck in replay mode in my head. *Shrink*. The way Uncle Jim said it, it doesn't sound completely out of reach. In fact, it sounds, well, doable.

Shrink. Maybe I can.

CHAPTER 13
When the Money Runs Out

I peek into Dad's new room at exactly four o'clock.

My dad is nowhere to be seen, but some guy is putting what looks like small hand weights into a cupboard under the sink. He turns around and smiles at me.

"Hey, you must be Bennett." He sticks out his hand. "I'm Jameel."

Jameel is tall, thin, and dark skinned, with large eyes and an even larger forehead. But he only looks to be in his late twenties or so. He's dressed in a T-shirt that says BURN CARBS, NOT GASOLINE. A small diamond sparkles from his left earlobe.

"I'll be working with your dad in the afternoons, so I'll probably be the guy you see the most. Your dad's just finishing up with his speech therapist. He should be back any minute."

Something about this guy makes me feel calmer

about visiting my dad in this place. "So, what do you do with my dad, anyway?"

Jameel washes his hands in my dad's sink while he talks. "I'm his physical therapist. I've got to strengthen all the muscles that your dad lost control of when he had his stroke. Some are just really weak. Others need to actually be retrained since the stroke screwed up some of the pathways from your dad's brain to his muscles."

Jameel grabs for a paper towel.

"What do you start with?" I ask. I sink onto the edge of my dad's bed. There are so many things I want my dad to be able to do again: talk clearly, use a fork, walk, slap me five.

"This week," Jameel says, pulling up a chair, "we're working on getting his hand muscles back so he can feed himself again. Then we'll tackle some of the larger muscle groups, like his legs and arms. It takes a while, and it's not going to be easy. But we'll get there."

Not easy. But possible. Kind of like what Uncle Jim said about losing weight.

"How long does it usually take?"

Jameel tilts his head and shrugs. "With some patients, it takes weeks. With others, it takes months. For some, it takes years. The more motivated he is, the better. What you can do is keep encouraging him, keep visiting him, and don't do things that'll slow down his progress, like bringing in candy bars or watching TV with him when you could take him for a walk. Do you get me?"

I nod.

"Will my dad ever be like, well, like totally himself again?" I ask, not sure if I'm ready to face the answer.

"That's a tough one, my friend. I'm not going to lie to you. Not all stroke patients recover. We can get him to a place where he can survive in everyday life and probably even go back to work. . . . Your dad's a project manager, right? In construction?"

"Yeah."

"Pretty good chance he can do that again at some point since it doesn't involve a lot of physical labor. But will he ever be completely like he was before? Probably not. Your dad's brain took a heavy hit when that stroke occurred. We can jog some of it back to life, but some of it is gone for good. There may be things he won't remember, ever."

My mind starts spinning. Will he remember my birthday? Our camping trips? Will he remember Mom? I feel as if I've taken a punch to the gut. I guess I've been assuming that the man I'd take home at the end of all this would be the same Dad I've always known.

A woman in khaki pants and a short-sleeved white shirt pushes a wheelchair into the room. My dad is sitting up in it. His head flops a little to the left, and his mouth looks kind of droopy: the way it does when the dentist gives you too much numbing medication. But his eyes are alert. As I approach his chair, he attempts a smile.

"Hey, Dad." I reach in to squeeze his shoulder. I try to smile back, but the conversation with Jameel still haunts me.

Jameel shakes out his long limbs and stands up.

"Listen, Bennett, I don't want you to be afraid to ask anything. You can call me here at the center if anything ever comes up, okay? Seriously, you're a key player in your dad's recovery. Paul, I'll see you tomorrow, my man." He reaches over and sticks out a closed fist toward my dad.

With painstaking slowness, my dad lifts his right arm, and his loosely curled fingers jab the air toward Jameel's hand. But he misses by about two inches.

"Dude." Jameel grins. "We gotta work on that!" He picks up my dad's hand, molds his fingers into a fist, and presses it against his own. "That's more like it!" My dad sighs, but it's a good-natured sigh.

I have a feeling Jameel is going to be very good for my dad.

The hour passes quickly, with me jabbering away and nothing to distract us. Dad looks tired enough to nod off, but I can tell he doesn't want to miss one of the few minutes he has with me. By the time Uncle Jim arrives at five, my dad's barely holding on to consciousness. I hug him quickly and follow my uncle to his car.

We're heading straight to my old house; I haven't been back there since right after my dad's stroke.

The house is stifling hot. I drag in the mail, pull out

some bills for Uncle Jim, and toss most of the rest. I grab my old sneakers since I'm doing all this walking in the mornings now. I poke through my closet and shove a few more T-shirts and jeans into a duffel bag, along with a couple of books that my dad had bought me before his stroke but that I hadn't read yet.

For my dad, I grab some shirts and pants, his pillow, a razor, stuff like that. The more he's able to move around, the more he'll want his own things around him. Or at least that's what I hope.

"Hey, sport, did you hear this message from your aunt Molly?" Uncle Jim calls from the living room.

I head out to see my uncle leaning over our answering machine, holding a pencil.

"What'd she say?"

"She wants you to call her more often with updates on your dad."

I make a mental note to text my aunt later that night. She's been calling a lot, and I've only talked to her once or twice. With Aunt Molly, a text is better than a phone call since she's been known to talk my ear off for a good forty-five minutes.

"There's also a message here from some guy at your dad's work. I'll try to call him this week. And somebody wants you to donate money to the Democratic Party."

I roll my eyes.

Uncle Jim looks at the pad of paper in front him and then back up at me uncomfortably. "Actually, there's one more message that we should talk about. Come sit down for a minute."

I follow him over to the couch. We sit across from each other. Whatever he has to tell me, he's not excited to do it. My palms grow sweaty.

"I debated telling you this; and honestly, your aunt doesn't know that I am. But I think you're old enough to be told the truth about this stuff. So here it is in a nutshell: There are some problems with your dad's insurance coverage."

"What?"

He's looking at me intently, his hands clasped between his legs. He leans forward to rest his elbows on his knees. "Insurance will only cover twenty-one days of your dad's rehabilitation."

It takes a second for me to process this. Then my stomach flip-flops.

"That's insane!" My heart's pounding, and my body has gone all rigid.

Uncle Jim holds up a hand. "Hang on, let me finish. After those twenty-one days are up, they'll pay a portion of the cost; but your dad is required to provide a co-payment."

I lean forward and swallow hard. "Okay. How much is the co-payment?"

Uncle Jim's eyes slide away for a second, and I know that it's not good news. "One hundred and seventy-five dollars per day."

My mind goes into math mode. Oh, God. That's twelve hundred dollars a week. Five grand a month.

"Do we have that kind of money? I mean, we have like a savings account, right?"

Uncle Jim takes a deep breath and shakes his head. "Not a lot. I'm guessing it was pretty much depleted when your mom got sick. And it seems like maybe your dad hasn't been able to build it back up a whole lot."

My brain is trying to process all this, but the enormity of the cost is staggering.

"So then, what are the options? A loan or something?" I'm feeling frantic. There have to be options, right?

"We could try to sell your house. Your aunt looked into that, but it could take a while and . . ."

"No." I stand up in a flash, no small feat for a walrus-sized kid. I look around my living room. Shake my head. "No. There has to be something else. I'll get a job or something."

Uncle Jim chuckles, but it isn't a happy chuckle. "Bennett, you're thirteen. That's not going to happen. But hang on a second, okay? We're looking into cashing out some of your dad's retirement savings. It's not the best option, but it's a possibility." I drop back onto our couch. Uncle Jim looks down at his hands. He's squeezing them together.

"There's one more thing, Bennett."

I brace myself, tightening my fists like I can somehow ward off this blow I know is coming.

"Your dad has to show signs of improvement. Every day. The rehabilitation center has to prove it's working, you know? That your dad's getting better every day by being there. Otherwise, they stop paying altogether."

"Seriously?"

My uncle nods. "And even if he improves, they'll only pay the partial amount for ninety days. Then you either start paying the full amount, or he comes home. As is."

Ninety days. Three months. That'll bring us to just before Christmas. Nobody wants Dad to be better and home by Christmas more than I do. But I think of the man in the wheelchair who can't even give Jameel a fist bump. Who can't speak. Can't eat yet. Will three months be enough?

"Does my dad know this?" I ask.

Uncle Jim shakes his head. "I don't think so. He's given control of everything to me and your aunt right now."

I breathe a sigh of relief. Dad doesn't need to worry about this.

"Does my dad still have a job?" I ask, my voice shaking.

"Thankfully, yes. They put him on disability for six months; and, hopefully, he can return to work after that."

I nod slowly.

"But without rehabilitation, the chances of your father being ready for work in six months are slim. There's the rub."

"So it's a no-win?" I say. "No rehabilitation, no work. No work, no insurance. No insurance, no chance for rehabilitation. Wow. This really, really sucks."

"Yeah. It does."

"There's nothing we can do? Sue them or some-thing?" I ask, feeling angry and helpless all at once.

"We can petition them for an extension. We can talk to your dad's employer, which is what I'm going to do on Monday. Or we can find some wealthy, generous person to pay for his therapy. Know anybody?"

I want to laugh. *Yeah,* I think bitterly, *my life is full of rich dudes who will fork over a bunch of money if I smile and say please.*

I drop my head into my hands. So this is how it works, huh? Real life.

It sucks.

CHAPTER 14
Cross-Country Flyer

The insurance nightmare should probably be consuming my every waking thought. But it isn't. I have other things to worry about. Namely Luis.

I'm not looking forward to lunch. I have a feeling Luis is the kind of guy who won't easily forget the piece of cake he demanded. He's not going to get that I've had no chocolate *anything* for almost a week now.

I'm also a little nervous about English. Seeing Taylor yesterday brought on a round of sweating. I want to play it cool. But that's not usually a strength of mine.

When I sit down third period, though, she offers me a bright smile.

"Hey, Bennett." We both drag out our homework and books.

"Hey, Taylor."

"You write your essay last night?" she asks, and digs a pen out of her bag. Taylor has the same long, straight hair as Kiley, but that's where the similarity ends. Taylor actually looks at me without the I-sucked-on-a-lemon expression.

"Yeah. You?"

She glances at me. Her chestnut-colored hair falls lightly across her face. She tucks it behind an ear absently. "Yeah. Wasn't so bad. I don't mind writing, actually."

"Me, either. What'd you write about?"

We'd been told to choose a person who means a lot to us or who we respect and do a "character sketch" of them, which I assumed meant use a lot of description.

"I wrote about this girl who lives next door to me. She has cerebral palsy. It really makes it hard for her to get around and do normal things; but she has the most amazing attitude, you know? It's like she's just decided she can do anything, and she's not going to let her condition stop her."

"She sounds pretty cool," I answer. Here I am having a real conversation with a girl. *Please don't let me have armpit sweat stains,* I think. "Be cool to meet her someday." *Oh, God! Did I just say that?*

"Yeah." Her green eyes slide away from mine. "Who'd you write about?"

"Um, well, I wrote about my mom." I blush. "She, um, well, she died when I was five."

"That must have been really hard," Taylor says, her brow furrowing. "I can't imagine losing my mom. That sucks."

"Yeah." I look away and then add something I've never said out loud. "I wish I'd gotten to know her better before she died. I feel like she was taken away before I could really find out who she was." I force myself to look back at Taylor. She's totally focused on what I'm saying. "So anyway, I thought I'd write what I did know about her so I'll at least have that for when I get old and can't remember to put my teeth back in every morning."

Taylor chuckles, flashing a dimple I'd never noticed before, and I swear the room gets brighter.

Then the bell rings and class starts. But I suddenly have hope that the day—no, the *year*—will be okay. Maybe Luis won't be as big a jerk as he was yesterday.

And maybe we'll have a light snowfall to cool us down by lunch. Shyeah, right.

• • •

P. G. and I decide to meet at our same spot on the wall. Unfortunately, Luis's whole gang is there again. He's already being an idiot, pulling his pants up really high and making everybody laugh at some poor sixth grader who happens to be strolling by.

I pull out my lunch, trying to ignore Luis and his obnoxious friends.

P. G. is attacking his cold tortillas, *machaca* beef, and salsa, his cheeks bulging with what I know is delicious food. My stomach rumbles.

In comparison, my lunch sucks. Turkey sandwich (on wheat), bottled water, an apple, a handful of vanilla wafers, one plain rice cake. If Luis is looking for chocolate cake in this lunch, he's about to be extremely disappointed.

Two bites into my sandwich, Luis strides over.

"Where's my cake, *gordo*?" He lifts his chin.

"Sorry, man, no cake today. My aunt's a health nut." I look at him, but I end up squinting because the sun's behind him.

"I told you to bring me cake."

The A.B.s have stopped talking now and are looking at us, sliding a bit farther away on the wall in case it gets messy.

"Hey, man," P. G. says. "Leave him alone, okay? He's got no cake. He doesn't even have anything good to eat—it's all, like, healthy crap. Let it rest."

"I'll let it rest when I get my cake." Luis snatches my lunch bag from me and dumps it out on the ground. The apple rolls back between my legs.

"Fat Boy's on a diet," he says to his groupies. "You trying to slim down for the ladies?"

"Well, it ain't for the guys," I say, hoping to keep it light.

"Heh-heh." He laughs forcibly. "You think you're funny, eh? Let's see if you're still so funny after PE today. See you in the locker room, Fat Boy." He saunters back to his little group.

I pick up the apple from the ground, wipe it off, and bite into it, my hand shaking slightly. P. G. finishes the last of his tortillas and tosses his brown bag. Neither of us speaks.

A few minutes later we head down toward the library. P. G. needs to find a book for English.

While he pulls out book after book, looking for the one that has the fewest pages, I wander over to the bulletin board, where the librarian hangs all the school news flyers. Honor Society is starting up. I make a mental note of the first meeting time. There's some stuff about the first dance in a week or so, which I don't even bother to read. Student government elections are coming up. Tryouts for the school play. Christian Club. Homework Club. Cross-country practice.

I stop for a second. I have no idea why, but I find myself reading the flyer carefully.

Cross-country season starts next Tuesday. Meet behind the gym after school for an introductory meeting and a quick run. Must have good running shoes, but no prior running experience needed. All are welcome.

The coach is some guy I don't know: Coach Mendoza. *What if . . . ?*

Then my sanity kicks in. *You've got to be kidding,* I tell myself. *Cross-country?*

I can barely WALK two miles! How can I possibly be thinking about running in a race!

But something Uncle Jim said hits me: *Underneath all that fat is a kid who can succeed.* Cross-country is probably the last thing he meant. But really, can I do it if I want to?

"Hey, B.," says P. G. from behind me. "You thinking of trying out for cheerleading or what?"

"Yeah, I heard they need someone for the top of the pyramid."

"You want to crush all them hot chicks, man?" he says with a grin.

The bell rings and we part ways. But I turn quickly and look at that flyer again. Next Tuesday. I shake the thought from my head. *You're* loco, I tell myself. *Crazy.*

CHAPTER 15
Go—for—It

PE is fast becoming my least-favorite time of the day. Yep, worse than lunch.

By Friday we have to dress. This means one hundred and fifty sweaty boys, all changing as fast as they can, trying to show as little skin as possible and get out to the blacktop without being late.

That small, windowless locker room is truly nasty. Brown, stained, forgotten socks litter the floor along with deodorant cans, candy wrappers, half-drank water bottles, broken pencils, and crumpled-up homework. The smell is overpowering: body odor, rank shoes, deodorant spray, urine, and mold. Yeah, that's another reason everyone hurries.

I stuff my backpack under the wooden bench and reach for the lock on my locker. It's covered in something pink and sticky. Luis's handiwork, no doubt. I pick away at the sticky mess and flip through my three-number combination quickly. Dressing at warp speed means that fewer kids will see my rolls of belly fat. Love handles and "boy boobs" do not go over well in a school locker room.

I've just managed to pull on my shorts and am reaching for my shoes when he strikes.

"Fat Boy!" he yells loudly. He has to. The noise in the locker room has reached a painful level, made worse by Mr. Haynes, who keeps screaming at everyone to "shut up and hurry."

"Hey, Luis," I say casually. "Good to see you. Gotta run, though. Don't want to be late." I finish tying my shoes and grunt to a standing position.

"Don't want to be late," Luis says mockingly. "I got a present for you, Fat Boy."

And with that he flings something white and strappy toward me. It takes a second before I realize it's a bra—and by the looks of it, a training bra. He cackles and hops onto one of the benches. "Make sure you've got enough support for our run today, Fat Boy!" he yells through cupped hands. Then he hops down and zigzags his way through the crowd to wherever his locker is, thankfully not by mine.

A few kids stare. Others look away and pretend not to notice my humiliation. One kid laughs and says, "Dude, it's a bra!" *Brilliant observation, Einstein.*

I sigh miserably. I toss the bra down to the floor and skootch it under the bench with my foot. Yep, the locker room sucks. And this is just day three.

I'm predictably last on the run, though not alone, since Drew drags up the rear with me. Mr. Haynes jots down our gold medal–winning times on a clipboard and sends us over to be tested on sit-ups and push-ups. Drew squeezes out three sit-ups and two push-ups. I manage four sit-ups but not a single push-up. Even with Aunt Laura's healthy eating, I have no upper body strength.

Looking over at the rest of the class—the *normal-sized* kids who can jog without wheezing and do a push-up without collapsing—I wonder if I'm insane. Because I can't seem to get that cross-country flyer out of my head. And some secret, crazy, out-of-my-mind part of me wants to see if I can do it.

• • •

Jameel is just finishing up with my dad when I get to the rehab center that afternoon. My dad is sweating and looks as if he's run a marathon or something.

"Hey, Bennett!" Jameel greets me. "What's up, man?"

"Not much," I say. "How come my dad looks like he's done five rounds in a boxing ring?"

Jameel laughs. "That's probably what it feels like to him, too. Therapy is hard work, Bennett. It tires him out pretty good. But"—Jameel places his hand on my dad's shoulder—"your dad's moving in the right direction. He's got a little more range of motion in his arms and a little more strength in his hands. His stamina is improving every day."

I glance over at my dad, who is staring back at me as

if to say *See, your old dad's working hard.*

I try to hide how relieved I really feel. My dad doesn't know it, but he's got to show this kind of improvement if he wants to stay here with Jameel. His insurance company simply won't allow him to slack off.

I smile at Dad. "Want some water? You look a little thirsty."

My dad nods. Jameel high-fives us both and leaves, his head bopping to a song only he hears.

I get my dad a drink of water, holding his straw so he can sip it, and flip open a *Sports Illustrated.* I read him three different articles before I notice that he's starting to nod off in his chair. Looking at him, I'm surprised to feel my chest grow warm. And even more surprised to realize why. I'm proud of my dad. He's working hard to get back in shape. He's stepping up to the plate.

Maybe I can, too.

"Hey, Dad," I say suddenly, pushing the call button for a nurse to come and move him into bed. "What would you think about me trying out for the cross-country team?"

His eyes flip open, and he pulls his heavy head up a bit.

"It's crazy, I know," I say. "I'm still thinking about it. But it's kind of something I'd like to try. You know?"

He looks at me long and hard. I can see his brain working overtime. I know it's only been two weeks since his stroke, but I wish he could speak or even write what he's thinking. I sure could use his encouragement right now.

Not for the first time I feel this rush of self-pity. My dad can't even drink by himself, much less offer advice when I need it.

But then the most amazing thing happens.

His lips part, and he pushes out some garbled sounds.

I shake my head. "Can't understand, Dad, sorry."

He purses his lips in frustration. Then, slowly, he opens his mouth again.

What comes out is slurpy sounding and difficult to understand. But miraculously, I get it.

"Go—for—it."

CHAPTER 16
Cute Girl Calls Fat Boy

That night Aunt Laura drops me off at *casa de Gomez*. I'm still amazed that she didn't put up more of a fuss about me sleeping over at P. G.'s house. She just said, "Make sure you eat a decent meal, okay?" Oh, it's going to be a decent meal all right—if by *decent* she means delicious, high in fat, and sure to make me feel full and happy.

The Gomez family acts as if I'm a soldier returning from war. Mrs. Gomez makes my favorite meal: *carne asada* tacos, rice, and *horchatas*, which are Mexican drinks made of rice, almonds, cinnamon, and sugar. I'm close to slobbering while I dish up everything. We sit down knee to knee at their tiny little table and clasp hands.

"Dear heavenly Father," says Mr. Gomez softly, head bowed. "Thank You for this bountiful food. We thank You also for allowing Bennett to be with us tonight. We praise Your powers of healing and hope that You lay them upon Bennett's father. In Your precious name, Amen."

I'm touched by their prayer, truly; but the minute that *Amen* is said, I'm stuffing a tortilla with meat into my mouth like I haven't eaten in decades.

"How's your *padre*?" asks P. G.'s *abuela*, her watery eyes squinting at me.

"He's doing much better. He can use his hands a little now. I can kind of understand some of his words, too."

"*Bueno*," says Mr. Gomez, nodding while he chews.

We're all quiet. Then P. G.'s two oldest sisters come in, hollering at each other about gas money and who owes who what. Both of them tussle my hair before pulling up chairs and squeezing into the already-packed table. The noise level hits just about painful once more, and all is right with the world.

• • •

I crash on P. G.'s floor. It's about midnight, and the house settles quickly into silence. We turn off the lights. Soon, though, P. G. props up on one elbow and looks at me.

"I'm thinking of asking Miranda to the dance," he says quietly.

I'm surprised. We've never gone to a dance, much less asked a girl to go with us.

"My sisters keep telling me to do it. That I need to, you know, take a risk. I think they might be right. How am I ever going to get Miranda to like me if she only sees me in English, where I suck?"

I nod. He has a point.

"Why don't you come, too, Benny-man? We could hang

out together and protect each other when we get mobbed by all the beautiful women."

I laugh. "I'll think about it."

"How's Taylor?" he asks.

"Out of my league." I fold my hands behind my head and look up at the ceiling.

"Oh, really? What'd she say again when you told her about your dad?" His voice rises an octave or so. "*Aw, poor Bennett!* She's got it bad for you, *amigo!*"

"Naw," I say, chuckling. "She's just being nice."

"You gotta come to the dance. What if she's there and you're not and some other guy asks her to dance?"

The thought of me dancing with Taylor makes my stomach flip-flop; but the thought of her dancing with someone else definitely feels worse. Still, I can't imagine touching her, much less swaying with her on a darkened dance floor. My stomach starts feeling swishy. I have to blink that thought away.

"Hey, Bennett," P. G. says seriously. "What're you gonna do about Luis, man? You can't keep taking his crap, you know."

"Yeah, I know." Truthfully? I really just planned to keep taking his crap . . . until he stopped giving it. Eventually, he'd find some other poor guy to torture, right?

"You gotta stand up to him," P. G. says. "He'll back off if you show him you aren't gonna take it."

"You think?"

"Yeah. I know his type. Underneath all that 'I'm the

man' stuff, he's a scared little bully hoping no one messes with his house of cards. Push one card and they all fall, bro. He'll back down. Seriously."

"Yeah, maybe," I say. But I'm not so sure. If I try to push back, Luis might double his efforts to screw with me.

P. G. yawns. "Plate time, dude."

Within minutes he's snoring softly.

Maybe he's right, though. Maybe it is plate time.

• • •

Saturday morning my aunt picks me up from P. G.'s and drops me at the rehab center. Jameel isn't there, but a young nurse named Al (short for Alexis) is. She has a red bandanna over her head of tight black curls and a small tattoo of a four-leaf clover on her ankle.

My dad is suspended in a harness over what looks like a treadmill. A robot-looking thing with arms is attached by straps to the outside of his legs. The robot moves, making my dad's legs move like he's walking.

"This machine will not only retrain the brain to send out signals to your dad's legs," explains Al, "but it'll also strengthen his muscles and improve his circulation."

"Very cool," I say.

Al helps my dad out of the harness and settles him back in his bed.

"Looking good, Dad."

He gives me a tired smile.

I flop into a chair and flip open a book I've brought

to read to my dad. It's by John Wooden, a legendary basketball coach at UCLA.

"Dad, want me to read a little?" I ask softly. He nods weakly and closes his eyes.

I start off slowly, reading about a basketball player coming off the court after a tough game. Moments later, I can hear Dad's soft little snore. I return to Wooden's book and am lost in the story within minutes.

John Wooden has always been one of my dad's heroes. "Not just a great coach," Dad would say whenever his name came up, "but a top-notch guy."

As I read, I begin to realize what my dad was talking about. His whole message seems to be that success isn't necessarily about winning. It's more about finding satisfaction in knowing you've given it everything you've got.

For a second I lower the book to my lap and gaze out the window. I haven't been able to make a decision about cross-country. Mostly because I'm kind of scared to think about what might happen if I actually show up in running shoes on Tuesday. What if I try—I mean, give it absolutely *everything* I have—and still fail? Will I find any satisfaction in that? Or would I simply be the laughingstock of Truman Middle School?

I sigh and grab the book to read until it's time to go.

● ● ●

Uncle Jim picks me up around lunchtime, and we head over to my house for another quick visit. He needs to gather some insurance papers, and I want to get some clothes I can run in (in case I actually decide to go on Tuesday).

Somebody—probably my aunt—has cleaned the place a little. Washed some dishes. Dusted. Straightened up things. The mess in the living room is gone. I can't decide if this is very thoughtful or very irritating.

Uncle Jim checks our voice messages while I give the front yard a quick watering. The few scraggly rosebushes we have are starting to look even more pathetic than usual.

Uncle Jim comes out on the front porch and watches me.

"So, Bennett?" Uncle Jim looks at me with raised eyebrows, his eyes twinkling. "You know somebody named Taylor?"

I feel my face getting warm.

"Yeah. She's a girl from school." I keep my eyes focused on the stream of water from the hose. "Why?" My heart is pounding.

"She left her number for you. Said to call her."

"Probably about homework in English or something."

Uncle Jim's smile nearly reaches both ears. I can feel the warmth in my face, red-hot now.

"Sure. Right. Homework in English." He hands me a

piece of paper. "Here's her number. Good luck, sport."

I stick the piece of paper in my pocket and walk over to turn off the hose.

I don't care if it is just about homework. Taylor looked up my number and called me. In the history of the world, this has never happened before. Cute Girl calls Fat Boy. Who would believe it?

And would he have the courage to call her back?

CHAPTER 17
The Longest Mile Ever

I spend Sunday doing homework and hanging out with my dad. One of the nurses helps me load him into his wheelchair, and we take a walk outside. Though he's lost some weight, my dad's still a big guy. Pushing him leaves me winded and sweaty. But I can tell he enjoys getting out of his room.

Dad can only say one or two words at a time, and they're mostly slurry and garbled. But we manage to communicate somehow. The effort of it all sometimes leaves me wiped out, though.

That night Josh and I take the trash cans out to the street for pickup the next day. I break down and tell him about cross-country. I haven't said a word to anyone except my dad, and I really want someone else's opinion.

"I think you should do it. Definitely," he says. "I'm sure there will be other kids who've never run before."

"You don't understand, Josh. I'm the kid who always

comes in last when we run. Last! And that's in PE class, where you have kids who don't like to run or, you know, girls who refuse to run. And I *still* come in last."

"Then you can only get better." He bangs a lid on one of the cans. "If you don't try, then how do you know if you can do it or not?"

I want to slug him. He can't possibly know what it feels like or where I'm coming from. But he looks so sincere that I drop it.

Monday morning at 6:30 on the nose I lace up the closest thing I have to running shoes. I throw on my iPod and stagger down the stairs, half asleep. I let myself out the side door. I've been walking for a week now, since last Sunday. These days I'm walking solo; Uncle Jim usually heads out a half hour before me. Sometimes he passes me as he runs. Today I plan to be running when he comes by.

It's going to be hot. There's already a warm wind blowing in from the desert. I adjust the earphones. I look up at the swaying palm trees. I've grown to love this time of the morning, even if it means dragging myself out of bed early.

I start with a fast walk. My aunt lives in a valley between a bunch of small mountains. This means there's basically no such thing as a flat street. No matter where you start, you have to go up a hill at some point.

I personally like to get my uphill done first and finish going downhill. So with that in mind, I head north up the street, walking at a brisk pace. By the last hundred yards it's pretty steep and I'm huffing. But I'm determined. At the top of our street I turn and head slightly downhill. There, I start my jog.

Keep breathing, I tell myself.

In and out. In and out.

After about one minute, any effort to control my breathing is gone. I'm sucking in air like the world's going to run out soon. Still, I keep running.

I make it a quarter mile before I stop. I'm gulping air, and my stomach heaves with each gasp. My calves are on fire, and my thighs feel as if someone has them in an iron grip. I take a long swig from the water bottle I'm carrying. I pant my way through the next minute, just standing there on that street corner.

Then I turn the corner and let gravity help me out. It's a nice steady downhill for about half a mile. I'm running so slowly that an old guy with a cane—probably out for his morning stroll—is having no trouble keeping up. But I'm running.

Everything hurts. My body feels like it weighs two tons. My feet feel as if they're slogging through mud. My chest is tight. But something won't let me stop. And amazingly, that part feels good.

At the next corner, with about a quarter mile to go, I stop again and suck in air. Guzzle more water. Do some quick stretches to relieve the pain in my legs. And then— feeling a little light-headed and woozy, but wanting this more than anything I've ever wanted in my life—I make my feet move again.

Every step hurts. Every breath is too small.

With one block left I'm like a zombie. There's a humming in my ears that isn't from my iPod. Sweat burns my eyes and stains my shirt. And around my belly button? A rapidly growing sweat stain you could probably swim in.

Suddenly Uncle Jim is beside me.

"Bennett! You're running! Amazing!"

His smile and the pride in his eyes snap me out of my misery. I'm going to run the rest of the way, even if it means puking on my uncle's Nikes.

By the time we hit our driveway, I'm shuffling along so slowly, a crawling baby would have been able to keep up. My heart races, and my body feels both warm and cold at the same time. I look down at my watch. Twenty minutes. I've run about a mile, maybe a tiny bit more, in twenty minutes. And I feel as if I've just set the world record.

"Bennett Robinson!" Uncle Jim shouts, pulling his ear buds out of his ears. "Did you really run? Was that *you* running?"

He sticks out a fist, and I tap it with my own, grinning foolishly and trying not to throw up.

"How far did you go?" he asks.

"About. A. Mile," I gasp, wiping sweat from my face with the bottom of my shirt, not caring if anyone sees my flabby belly.

"That's incredible! I'm so proud of you, sport!" He claps me on my sweaty back. "What got into you?"

"Just . . . wanted . . . to see . . . if I could do it." I'm feeling a little better. I gulp some more water.

"It won't be long before you're beating me home." He grins. "What a great way to start this day. Good job, Bennett. Now, go take a shower, boy; you stink!"

I laugh, already feeling ten pounds lighter and thinking maybe I really *can* do this. I can't wait to tell my dad.

Unfortunately, my morning tanks quickly once I get to school. In English, Taylor is acting weird, and I have no clue why.

"Hey, Taylor," I say all friendlylike as I sit down at our table. "How was your weekend?"

"Fine," she says stiffly, not looking me in the eye.

Is this the same girl I sat next to last week? Who chatted with me like we were old friends from way back?

I try again.

"Hey, I was wondering if you've ever read anything by Walter Dean Myers? He's got this great book about Harlem I think you'd like."

"Nope, never heard of him."

Okay, so I may not be, like, Romeo with the girls; but I can read signals, and this girl is telling me to get lost. I don't get it. She called me, right? Left a message? Was it to tell me to get lost? To leave her alone?

She doesn't get any warmer as class goes on. When we break up into groups to discuss a poem, she pretty much only talks to the other two people in our group and won't look at me.

I'm stumped. I check my shirt for some embarrassing stain and breathe into my palm, wondering if my breath is bad. I can't imagine what I've done. I want to ask, "Hey, Taylor, did I do something to make you mad?" But that would require what P. G. calls *el coraje*, and I have none. When the bell rings, she grabs her backpack and leaves quickly, without saying good-bye.

All too soon it's lunchtime.

That morning I'd asked P. G. if we could sit somewhere else at lunch. He'd looked at me good and hard and then said no.

I was a little tweaked. Why was he pushing this?

Luis makes it a point now to check my lunch every day to see if I'm sticking to my "diet." If he likes something, he takes it. If it wasn't for Aunt Laura's healthy, unappealing lunches, I'd go hungry.

Today when Luis comes to grab my lunch, I try a new tactic. "Hey, man, can you just let me eat my lunch today?"

No dice.

He makes his "Fat Boy" comments louder than usual and "accidentally" drops everything but my sandwich in the trash.

P. G. wordlessly hands me a cold chimichanga. I feel the crushing weight of my friend's disappointment.

We sit in silence for a few minutes before I finally speak.

"You ask Miranda to the dance?"

"Yeah." He doesn't sound too excited.

"What'd she say?"

"She's got other plans."

"Sorry, man."

"No biggie." He shrugs.

But it is a big deal. Makes me glad I didn't ask Taylor. I don't need that kind of rejection right now. Of course, neither does P. G. I try to think of something to say to cheer him up.

Nothing comes.

In PE, Luis has taped a Jenny Craig ad to my locker and smeared what looks like butter all over the handle, making it nearly impossible to grip and open it. Across the ad is the word *LARDO* in big red marker. I rip it down fiercely. He's getting harder to ignore.

P. G. is right. If this is going to last until June, I have to do something. But what?

• • •

That afternoon I ask Aunt Laura to drop me at my dad's right after school. I know I'll have to wait to see him, but that's okay. I have the John Wooden book, my iPod, and my phone. What more could I need? Okay, a Butterfinger would be nice. This new place he's in has no vending machines. I haven't had a Twinkies fix in almost a week now.

I sit outside for about a half an hour reading and watching other rehab patients walk with the nurses under the shade of the palm trees. I make a quick call to my aunt Molly, who tells me to hug my dad for her and that she's going to try to get some time off to come see him. Finally, at exactly four, I go in.

"Hey, your dad's kicking butt, my man!" Jameel exclaims when he sees me. He looks proudly over at my dad, who's in his favorite chair by the window. He's sitting straighter today. I can tell something's up.

"What'd he do?" I ask.

"He fed himself lunch today, that's what!" Jameel says, and grins.

My dad nods.

"Way to go, Dad!" I shout, and go over to hug him. He looks so pleased sitting there. I can tell he's trying to talk, so I wait patiently.

"App . . . le . . . sowce," he says, each syllable a triumph.

"Nice!" But my heart drops for a second, thinking about the whole insurance thing. These little victories aren't just cool—they're mandatory. If he's going to stay here, he's got to progress from applesauce to cutting his own steak pretty quickly.

I paste a smile on my face, anyway.

"And I have some news for you," I say.

Jameel turns around. "Can I get in on this action, too?"

I sort of shrug, but secretly I'm pleased he's interested. "I've been walking every morning before school. But this morning I really wanted to see if I could push a little harder. So I walked the first half mile and then . . ." I pause and tap my fingers on the table in a drum roll, even though I know it's corny. "I ran the last mile!"

My dad's eyes widen, and he slowly holds up a hand for me to slap. I have to grab it before I slap it or the force of my hand hitting it might knock it completely off. But that's okay; he's tired from a long day, and at least he's trying.

"Bennett, that's sweet!" Jameel says, and high-fives me. "Good for you! That had to have been smokin' hard."

"Yeah. I wanted to quit. But I didn't. It took me almost twenty minutes to run only a mile. Grandma Jean would've beat me. But I did it."

My dad's eyes are glistening the tiniest bit, which makes me feel pleased but uncomfortable, too. Before his stroke, I never saw my dad cry, even when my mom died. But then, I never saw him fall face-first into the coffee table before, either. We crossed that line together; maybe it's time to cross more.

"Gggrrrreat . . . job."

"Well, rock on, future marathon runner," Jameel remarks with a smile. "I'm out of here."

I spend the next hour jabbering about school and other stuff. I tell Dad about Aunt Molly coming to visit and even fill him in on Taylor, something I probably wouldn't have done in our prestroke life. But when you have exactly one hour to spend each day with your dad and he basically hangs on your every word, you get pretty brave about opening up.

He asks me, in his slurry, hard-to-understand way, if I'm going to do cross-country. I shrug. Then he surprises me by telling me—in halting, one-word sentences—that my mom ran cross-country in high school. I don't say anything, but I'm suddenly wondering if this is a sign. A good sign.

Before I know it, it's five o'clock. The dinner crew comes in and scoots me out the door. I give my dad a last hug and head outside to wait for Uncle Jim.

As I stand there, I realize that even with his slurred speech bursts, even with his sagging lip and semiuseless limbs, I enjoy being with my dad. He doesn't have to be perfect or have the perfect body for me to love him.

I know *I* don't have the perfect body. But I'm a pretty decent guy. Could Taylor maybe somehow see that? And if so, then why is she treating me like dirt?

There's only one way to find out. I still have the little sticky note that Uncle Jim wrote her number on. In fact, I've stared at it so many times I have it memorized. I once even punched the seven digits into my cell phone, but chickened out before hitting the call button. But the digits are there, stored in my "dialed calls" file.

Mustering my determination from this morning, I find her number and hit CALL. I'm outside the building now, getting good reception and praying Uncle Jim will be a few minutes late.

"Hello?" It sounds like her, but I'm not sure.

"Hi, is Taylor, uh, there, please?" I ask, my heart hammering.

"This is Taylor." Thank God I don't have to go through her parents.

"Hey, it's Bennett. From English. We sit at the same table."

She laughs. "I know who you are, Bennett. What's up?"

She sounds okay, even friendly. I dive in, praying the water won't be cold.

"Well, you seemed a little, um, angry at me today; and I wanted to make sure we were cool. And you had called and left a message at my house, which I didn't get until this weekend because I'm not living there right now. So I'm kind of returning your call, too." *Breathe, Bennett.*

"I ... well ..." She sighs. "Yeah, I had a rotten morning — my mom was being ... difficult. And, well, actually, I was a little irritated that you hadn't called me back, I guess. I totally forgot you weren't at your house."

I kick myself mentally for not calling her back sooner. Somehow, I have to find some confidence. Maybe this is a start.

"Anyway, I'm watching my neighbor this Friday night," Taylor says. "She's a few years younger than us, but with the cerebral palsy, remember? Her mom likes her to stay with someone rather than be alone. So she's coming over to hang out; and, I don't know, I was wondering if you wanted to come hang out with us. Meet her. And she could meet you."

Is this for real? Taylor wants to hang out with me. No, really, TAYLOR WANTS TO HANG OUT WITH ME!

This has to be the absolute best day of my life. I look up toward the sky and think, *I won't mark off the days, Mom. But how about noting the really cool ones?*

"I would like that," I say, more honestly than I've ever said anything. "I'll see you tomorrow in class, okay? And, hey, no more cold shoulder, right?"

"Deal." She laughs.

We hang up. I sit on the bench and start digging around in my backpack for a packet of Oreo cookies I'd bought at school and was saving for an emergency. Maybe this isn't an emergency, but it sure qualifies as a celebration.

I'm ripping open the package and am about to grab the first cookie when I freeze. I think about this morning—running—and how good it felt (when it was over, anyway). I picture my dad lifting a shaky spoon of applesauce to his mouth. And my uncle Jim saying "Shrink."

I can do it. I can shrink. But not like this. Not by sneaking Twinkies and Oreos every chance I get.

I squeeze the package hard in my fist, feeling the cookies crumble. Then, before I change my mind, I toss the package into the trash can nearby. I hear its hollow thump as it hits the bottom.

And I smile.

CHAPTER 18
The Cross-Country Question

To run or not to run, that is the question. A question that haunts me even in my sleep. Monday night I have this creepy dream.

I'm doing my usual leisurely morning lap around the block. All of a sudden I realize I'm running. *Really* running. The kind of running you see in the Olympics. My legs are totally flying, and I feel as if I should be winded or struggling, but I'm not. It feels awesome, like I can keep going forever.

Then I turn a corner and there's Taylor, walking on the sidewalk with her backpack on.

"Wow! Bennett!" she says, her eyes shining. "I didn't know you could run like that! You're amazing!"

I grin modestly but don't slow down to talk.

Around the next corner is my aunt Laura. "Bennett!" she calls. "You didn't eat a proper breakfast! You know my rule! You shouldn't be running like that! Bennett!"

I happily ignore her and speed past.

I'm beginning to think I can run forever when suddenly Luis appears, blocking my path.

"Fat Boy," he says, his eyes dark, "you can't run from me. You should know that. I'll always catch you."

And then, because I have actual *coraje* in my dreams, I stop and face him.

"You're wrong, Luis. I'm too fast."

He reaches out to push me, but I shrug from his grasp and turn to run. Only this time my Olympic speed is gone. My legs feel as if they're made of heavy bricks. Each step is painful. I look back over my shoulder in a panic, expecting to see Luis ready to beat the crap out of me.

Instead, it's my dad. He seems even more overweight than ever. He is slumped in an armchair, looking at me with sad eyes.

"Don't you see?" he says in a clear voice, though it's obvious from looking at his body that he's had his stroke. "We can't change who we really are, Bennett. And you and me? We're fat. We can't shrink. We're just fat."

I wake up with a heavy heart, the dream so clear in my head that it feels more like a memory. I lie awake for a while. Wrestling with the question of cross-country. Thinking of my mom. Did she run like I did in my dream: weightless and fast? Finally, I nod off again, but I toss and turn until the alarm clock wakes me.

It's Tuesday.

D-day. Time to make a decision.

I tie my shoes and wonder if I should bother running this morning. Uncle Jim warned me that I probably shouldn't push myself too hard.

"With your body like it is," he explained last night after dinner, "if you try to push it again tomorrow, you could struggle. Better to wait another day, give yourself time to recover, and try again."

He doesn't know about cross-country practice this afternoon unless Josh told him, and I highly doubt that.

I quietly let myself out the front door and decide to take my uncle's advice. Instead of running, I walk my normal two miles as quickly as I can, thinking a lot about my dad. He's been in rehab seven days. He's got fourteen more before we start paying—as long as he keeps improving, that is. I have to make sure he keeps improving.

After a way-too-fast shower, I shove my running shoes in my backpack. On our car ride, I tell Aunt Laura I have to meet with a teacher after school.

"It shouldn't be too long, maybe fifteen minutes after you normally pick me up?" I ask. I really don't want to tell her about cross-country practice in case I chicken out.

"Are you in trouble?" she asks, gazing at me in the rearview mirror.

Kiley's head whips around toward me. I swear she looks hopeful.

"No, no, nothing like that. I think she wants me to change groups or something. No big deal."

Aunt Laura sighs. Heavily. "Fine. But watch for me, please, because we'll be rushing to get you to your dad's on time."

I look over at Josh. He subtly gives me the thumbs-up sign and mouths, "Good luck."

Luis, mercifully, is absent from school—probably suspended or maybe skipping. The best five minutes of my day occur in English. Taylor smiles when she sees me. I sit down across from her and say, "Hey," and lean away from her with exaggerated caution, as if I expect her to hit me at any minute.

"Oh, stop!" She giggles.

Giggles? Is she . . . could she possible be . . . (holy Toledo, Batman!) . . . flirting with me? No, I refuse to even think those thoughts; it just raises the bar too high.

The bell rings, cutting off our conversation; but I catch her eye twice more during the period, and she smiles each time. She even rolls her eyes once and pretends to be falling asleep as our teacher goes on and on about some poem. I'm in serious happy mode by the time the class ends.

"She digs you, dude," P. G. says at lunch.

"Naw." I shrug. "She's just being nice."

"Really?" He looks at me out of the corner of his eye. "'Cause when a girl's just bein' nice to me, she picks up a pencil I've dropped or gives me an answer to a math problem. She doesn't invite me to her house to meet her neighbor and giggle with me in class. I'm telling you, dude, I know these things. That girl wants you."

This tiny bubble of joy works its way up my throat. I laugh.

"No Luis today," P. G. remarks casually a few minutes later. Too casually.

"Yeah." I concentrate on my turkey on wheat. "Nice, huh?"

"You could get rid of him, you know," P. G. says without looking at me. "Go toe-to-toe with him, and he'll crumble."

"I guess."

"You don't believe me?" P. G.'s normally deep voice rises in a challenge.

"It's not that I don't believe you." I won't look at him. "It's the toe-to-toe thing. You've heard the rumors, dude. A switchblade as big as a banana. Like, what would I do then?"

"He doesn't have no switchblade." P. G. shakes his head dismissively. "I bet he started that rumor just to freak everyone out. Looks like it's working."

We're both silent.

Only a few minutes until the bell rings and lunch will be over. Along with this conversation, I hope. I toss my trash and stand up.

"Uh, don't wait for me after school today," I say.

P. G. looks up from his cell phone. "You get detention?" he asks. His eyebrows arch in surprise.

I laugh. "You sound like my aunt. No, dude, I just have to . . ."

Suddenly, I don't want to tell him. What if he laughs at me? Or worse, what if I bail at the last minute? He's already pretty hacked at me about Luis. "I have to meet with my English teacher. She's got a book or something for me."

P. G. looks at me a second longer. I think he knows something's up and is deciding whether or not to press me about it.

"You sure this doesn't have to do with Taylor?"

"Dude, lay off the Taylor thing already! I just have to see this teacher about something."

P. G. hesitates. Then he shrugs and grabs his backpack.

"Okay, man. See you *mañana* then."

• • •

I am so wishing that all I have to do is meet with a teacher. It's plate time.

I fully plan to bolt if I see a crowd of long, lean runners all going out for cross-country. They'll take one look at me, burst out laughing, and tell me that the Future Food Critics of America Club is meeting in Room 203 and not behind the gym.

But Uncle Jim's words keep echoing in my head: *A kid who can succeed.* He thinks I'm that kid. I need to think so, too.

I walk out of the locker room into the bright California sunshine with my shoulders squared.

Only a handful of kids are standing around, some

chatting, some looking nervous like me. They all have on workout clothes and running shoes, and most of them are sixth graders. I sit on a bench near the locker room, ready to disappear when the real jocks start to arrive.

Except the coach shows up first. He begins walking around, chatting with every kid, and handing him or her a clipboard so they can sign up. I try to stay off to the side. Maybe he'll take one look at the fat kid in the corner and think there's no way I can possibly be planning to run cross-country. But he walks right up to me.

"Here for cross-country?" he asks easily. He doesn't even look me up and down. He looks right at my face. His pen is poised over his clipboard.

"Well, yeah, I think so." I take a breath. "I mean, I've never run cross-country before, but I've started running in the mornings and would like to try it." That isn't really a lie, right? More like an exaggeration?

"Great," he says with a warm grin. "What's your name?"

I give him my name, grade, and cell phone number, reluctant to give him Aunt Laura's. I don't want her to know yet. The thought of her pumping her fist in victory, knowing she helped to create the New-and-Improved Bennett, is not a pleasant thought.

Other kids arrive. And just as I suspected, most of them are athletic looking, with long legs and thin frames. But there is one kid who you could maybe call a "big girl." She's tall and a little heavy, but she looks fit. The others greet her enthusiastically, making it clear that she was on the team last year. There's also this other kid who isn't overweight but who looks about as nervous as I am. I walk over to him.

"Hey, what's up?"

He nods his head once.

"You run cross-country before?" I ask.

"No," he says anxiously. "This is my first time. Have you?"

"Nope. I'm new, too. What's your name?"

"Calvin. I just moved here, and my mom thought it would be a good way to meet people. But I'm not sure I'm a fast-enough runner. I don't really run all that much."

"Yeah, I hear you." Poor guy. He looks ready to jump out of his skin. "I'm Bennett, by the way."

The coach asks for our attention. Calvin and I sit on the concrete steps behind the gym. I breathe slowly, trying to avoid armpit—or worse, belly button—sweat stains when we haven't even run yet.

"First of all, I'm Coach Mendoza." He surveys us. "I'm glad you guys are here. It's good to see some of our returning runners. But I always love to see new faces, too. Some of you may not have run cross-country before. Doesn't matter to me."

Breathe, Bennett. He doesn't sound so bad. I look down. No armpit stains. Yet.

"All levels and abilities are welcome on this team. Some of you are seasoned runners, and you know what your PR is, and you know how to try to beat it. Some of you haven't run enough to achieve a PR. That's fine, too."

"PR"? I'll have to ask Uncle Jim about that one since I have no clue what he's talking about.

"I have one rule. Everybody runs; everybody finishes. That's all I ask. If you start a course, you finish, even if you have to walk or limp across."

That'll be me. Limping. Crawling. Puking my way across the line.

"Hey, Coach! Do you have to bring up the whole limping thing EVERY year?"

I look over at the kid who spoke. He's tall and thin, with long, muscular legs. He looks as if he could keep up with Uncle Jim, no problem.

Coach Mendoza chuckles. "Well, let's see, Mark. Would that be the run where you were dead last? I didn't think a human being could run that slowly. I was sure you were actually going backward!" The team laughs, and Mark is grinning.

"If I remember correctly, Mark," Coach says teasingly, "you set a new course record. Twenty-six minutes. The slowest anybody had ever run."

"Hey, man," Mark says good-naturedly. "It's just good to be in the record books."

Again the team laughs.

I wonder how Mark will feel when I steal his record.

"Anyway," says Coach, "let's run through the stuff you need to know about our season. First of all, we practice

Monday through Thursday from two thirty until three thirty. Some weeks we'll throw in a Friday practice as well. We won't necessarily run every one of those days; we'll want to condition some days."

"By *condition*," interrupts the heavy girl, "he means pain. Lots and lots of pain!"

The returners groan while we newcomers look around nervously. Pain? My right leg starts jiggling.

"Thanks, Kendra, for being the voice of encouragement! Yes, there is some pain involved. But it's not horrible. Anyway, folks, we have our first meet in two weeks; and we'll be done by the middle of October. I don't expect us to be in perfect shape by this first race, but the other schools won't be either, so we'll be fine."

Middle of October. Less than two months. Just a couple of weeks, really. How bad could anything be for just a couple of weeks, right?

"Finally, if you plan to show up for our first real practice tomorrow, I need this form right here . . ."—he holds up a piece of paper—"filled out and signed by your parents or guardian. Questions?"

My heart sinks. I'm going to have to tell Aunt Laura or at the very least Uncle Jim tonight if I am really going to do this.

Finally, Coach says he wants us to run a short and easy half mile so he can get a feel for how everybody runs.

"Nothing to stress about. Take it easy," he cautions. "Don't go hard or try to show off."

By "take it easy" I wonder if he means "leisurely walk." Probably not.

On the Coach's whistle, Calvin and I start slowly. We stay at the back of the pack. Soon, the pack sprints off, leaving us behind. It's a position I'm very familiar with.

The half mile goes slowly. Calvin stays with me for a few minutes, but I wave him ahead when it's obvious he can and wants to run faster. My muscles ache. I'm gasping at the end, even though I finish a good two minutes behind everyone else.

Coach Mendoza is at the finish line, shouting out times—mine is seven minutes and six seconds.

"Nice job!" he yells to me in the same tone he used with everybody else.

I'm standing to the side, drinking my water and trying to breathe normally when the girl I noticed earlier—Kendra—comes up to me.

I tense. Here it comes. The you-can't-possibly-think-you-can-run conversation.

"Hey," she says. "You ever run before?"

"Not much." I shrug.

"Yeah, I can tell." She laughs. "I think you're in my math class. You're friends with P. G., right?"

I nod. Now I'm really wishing I'd just gone home and forgotten this whole idea.

"When I started cross-country two years ago, I looked a lot like you. I was pretty overweight. Man, I tell you, the thought of running a half mile scared me to death! But I was tired of being the fat girl in class and decided I was going to do something about it."

My heart is pounding. It's like she's talking about me.

"I heard the cross-country team was really cool." She wipes sweat from her forehead. "This first run about killed me! And I almost quit. I was near tears. Then this girl came up to me and told me to stay with it. So that's what I want to tell you. Stay with it, okay? It gets easier. And Coach Mendoza's awesome."

She starts to walk off. I stop her. "Can I ask you a question?"

"Sure." She swigs from her water bottle.

"How fast did you run that half mile two years ago?"

"Hmm," she says, and thinks a minute. "Maybe seven minutes, something like that."

"And how fast did you run today?"

She grins. "Four minutes, forty-two seconds. And I'm a little out of shape from the summer."

Walking back to the locker room, I wonder what to do with the consent form. Ask my uncle to sign it? Or suck it up and ask my aunt? Actually, maybe my dad can sign it. It's not as if his signature was real recognizable before his stroke, so who cares if it's just a messy scribble now?

And then it hits me. I'm not questioning *if* I'm going to get it signed. I'm actually going to attempt this crazy idea of mine.

I can't wait to tell P. G.

CHAPTER 19
Loco P. G.

"**S**o, uh, joined the cross-country team today."

Josh grins.

"Seriously?" Kiley looks at me like I'm truly insane. And Aunt Laura's eyes narrow in the rearview mirror.

"You what?"

"He joined cross-country, Mom! Isn't that awesome!" Josh is grinning as if he just won the lottery.

"You? Really? Running?" Kiley's nose is wrinkled in disgust. It's actually kind of comical.

"That's where you were after school?" My aunt presses, her tone flat and unreadable.

I nod. Nervous.

"Why didn't you tell me that?"

Let's see . . . first, I can't stand you. Second, I can't stand you. And third, well, I can't stand you.

"I guess I didn't want you to know in case I decided not to do it at the last minute."

Josh glances over at me with admiration. He gets it.

"Well, I suppose I can understand that," Aunt Laura says.

The car is silent for a moment. Josh bumps me with his elbow and grins.

"So you're going to run cross-country," Aunt Laura finally says. "That's really exciting."

"Or completely wacked," Kiley mutters under her breath.

Aunt Laura shoots her a warning look. "We might have to celebrate this news."

Why does she make that sound about as much fun as going to the dentist?

"Can we have ice cream after dinner?" Josh asks.

"Ice cream isn't necessarily the best food for a training runner," she says. "But, okay, just this once."

"Um, Aunt Laura? One more thing," I say.

"You're pushing it," Aunt Laura says with mock exasperation.

"Can I get some new running shoes? These old ones I have are way too small."

"After the ice cream. Your uncle Jim will be thrilled with an excuse to stop at a running store."

• • •

My dad claps me on the arm when I tell him the news and shakily signs my form with some unidentifiable scribble. I grin while he does it and note that I was right: it doesn't look a whole lot different than it did before his stroke. It's nice to have found *something* that hasn't changed.

After dinner my aunt, uncle, and cousins all pile into the car, and we go for ice cream. It turns out to be the best hot fudge sundae I've ever had. Not only because I haven't had one in so long, but because of what it means. Plus, I'll burn it off, right? During training?

Our next stop is a running store. I run on a treadmill for about thirty seconds while the sales guy watches my feet intently. Apparently, he's looking for how much my foot rolls in or out when I run. He tells me I overpronate—meaning my foot rolls inward—which is not uncommon in overweight people.

The sales guy finds me a few pairs of shoes that will help correct that and also help me avoid shin splints, since they don't sound fun. I quickly find shoes that feel like gloves on my feet. Unfortunately, they cost more than a hundred dollars. Uncle Jim doesn't look even a little bit fazed.

"If you're going to do this, Bennett, then you need to have the right equipment. Your dad's been giving us money for you, most of which we haven't needed to spend. Please, let us all—your dad included—do this for you." I nod, afraid that if I speak I might cry and then look really dumb crying about running shoes.

Uncle Jim throws a Dri-Fit shirt at me as well, saying I'll need it to keep me cool. I can't believe they have one in my size, but I guess I'm not the only XXL runner out there.

Back at the house, Uncle Jim gives me an old watch of his that will tell me my distance, overall time, pace, and even how many calories I burn. He shows me how to set it up and how to use it. I place it next to my bed, ready to slap it on when that alarm goes off the next morning.

The last thing my uncle says to me before he leaves is "I'm really proud of you, sport. Not because you're running. But because you stepped out of your comfort zone. That's a big deal, Bennett. It takes courage."

I mumble an embarrassed thanks but feel like a million bucks. Then my phone rings.

"P. G.! You're not going to believe what happened, dude!" I launch into the whole thing about cross-country and the trip to the running store. I end with "Wait till I show you my shoes, dude! They're beast, man!"

There's silence on the other end. I pull my phone from my ear and check for reception. Still got all my bars.

"P. G.? You there?" I say when I put the phone back to my ear.

There's a long pause. "You really want to do this, man? You sure you can be a cross-country runner? If I remember correctly, you and me were crossing that finish line in PE together . . . last."

"But, P. G., wait." This isn't like him at all. "I've been running in the morning. Well, walking mostly, but running a little. And this girl on my team came up to me today and told me how she started out really slow. . . ."

"Oh, I get it." His tone is sharp. "It's *my team* now, huh? You've been to what, one practice?"

"No, I didn't mean that it's *my* team. You know what I meant. What's up with you, anyway? Something happen with Miranda?"

As soon as it's out of my mouth, I wish I could take it back. Miranda has been a sore subject for the last two days.

"I just don't think you should be getting your hopes up is all." There's an edge to his voice. "Kids like us, well, we don't run cross-country. I mean, you know I got your back, bro. But you're getting beat down pretty bad by Luis. What happens when you get crushed in your first race? You gonna be able to handle that?"

"But I've got to start somewhere, P. G." I can't believe this. I was so sure he'd be happy for me. "My dad just had a stroke, dude, because he's fat. I don't want that to happen to me. Or you."

"What're you saying, Bennett? You got a problem with my size all of a sudden?"

"No. That's not what I meant. You're not . . ."

"I'm happy with who I am." He's all ice now. "I don't need to lose weight to impress some chick in my English class."

"You think I'm doing this for Taylor?" A sick feeling is taking over my stomach.

"Oh, come on! It's pretty obvious, isn't it?"

"You think I'm doing this for Taylor," I repeat, blown away by how my best friend is acting. "Then you don't know me, P. G."

"Maybe not, bro. Maybe not." I hear him hang up.

I'm crashing down to earth. Hard.

I knew I'd have to do this without my dad around to cheer from the sideline. And for a while now I've had to do everything without the support of my mom. But without P. G.? It's unthinkable.

I look over at the beautiful new running shoes I've placed neatly under the desk chair in my room. At the Dri-Fit shirt that's supposed to keep the sweat off my body. And at the watch that will tell me how far I've run and how fast I've done it.

Does it really matter how far or how fast if your best friend isn't there to cheer you on?

Suddenly exhausted, I lie back on my bed and stare at the ceiling. I really think I want to do cross-country, but right now there are just so many things weighing me down.

Reaching over, I pull open the drawer of my nightstand. I feel around until my hand finds it: a king-sized Snickers bar that P. G. bought for me at school last week. I'd hidden it away, hoping to avoid temptation. Now I rip it open savagely and shove the biggest bite I can into my mouth.

In less than three minutes the wrapper is empty. But the ache in my body is still there.

I roll over onto my side and try to close my eyes. A

feeling of loneliness and loss, and guilt over the stupid Snickers bar, sweeps over me.

Can I patch this thing up with P. G. tomorrow? Explain why cross-country is so important to me and get him to understand?

"Plate time, Bennett," I whisper softly. But I don't sound ready. I sound like a wimp.

CHAPTER 20
Commitment

Luis is back in school the next day. I don't even have to wait until lunch before he's in my face with "Fat Boy" this and "Fat Boy" that. I pretend it doesn't bother me. That seems to irritate him more.

In science P. G. walks in right as the bell rings. He slumps into his seat and keeps his eyes glued on the teacher the whole period. He might as well punch me in the ribs. That's how it feels. When the bell rings at the end of class, I stand quickly, hoping to grab his attention. He's already halfway out the door.

"P. G.!"

He either doesn't hear me or ignores me. In seconds he's disappeared into the mass of students in the hallway.

At lunch I head straight to our spot on the wall. It's empty. So much for patching up things. I pull out my cell phone and punch in his number. Then I hesitate. Should I try to call him? Will he ignore the call?

He's totally overreacting, but maybe he just needs time to get used to the idea of me running cross-country. I slide my phone back into my pocket.

Spinning around, I head for the library. The librarian will let anybody eat in there if they're quiet and look as if they're reading or studying. I escape into my iPod and try to read, but I can't stop thinking about what happened yesterday. I nibble at my turkey sandwich before throwing the whole sack out.

As the minutes tick by, my anger grows. P. G. has no right to act like this. I haven't done anything wrong! How dare he say I can't run cross-country? That kids like me can't be athletes?

I think about this hard for a second. What if running is more than just a sport, something to do after school? What if it's even more than a way to lose weight? Maybe it's my way of standing up. It's me telling my dad, "I don't want to live a life of fast food. I don't want to be a couch potato anymore."

How could that be such a big deal to P. G.? How could that be wrong?

The bell rings, signaling the end of lunch. Sighing, I grab my stuff and head to fifth period.

At practice Coach Mendoza greets us all with two short whistles that mean "Get your butts running!" We do two laps around the blacktop as a warm-up. It's another blistering hot day. By the second lap I'm struggling.

I notice a few top runners have finished and are starting to stretch. The main pack is a good half lap ahead of me. Am I crazy for being out here? For trying to pretend to be an athlete? What was I thinking?

And in that second I want to quit. I mean, I'm way out of my league here. Plus, everything hurts. My feet and legs. My lungs. My shins. Even the new shoes are no match for this old body that's still mine.

Off in the distance I see someone who looks like P. G. walking toward the tree we usually wait under. His head is down, and his shoulders are turned inward. Seeing him saps what little energy I have left. I'm convinced that this is a huge mistake. I'll get through this first practice and then go back where I belong: with the other fat kids.

A few minutes later I shuffle up to the rest of my team. My head turns toward the tree. P. G. is gone.

Kendra and Mark stretch us out. Even that's hard. My thighs are about twice the size as everyone else's, so sitting cross-legged and reaching forward is like trying to fit a beach ball through a basketball hoop. You can push and shove, but unless you pop it with a pin, your chances of success are limited.

My chance of success is zero.

But nobody seems to notice or care that I'm as flexible as a tree trunk.

After that Coach gathers us around him and starts talking. Today we're going to run four laps around the track: a full mile. He'll time us, which will give him a baseline time for each of us for the season. Tomorrow, he says, we'll stay on campus and do some "fun" hill repeats to build our strength.

"The races at the meets are all two miles," he explains. "These couple of weeks are meant to get you in good enough shape to run that."

He goes on to say that we'll be doing some interval work (no clue what that means), hill repeats (that doesn't sound good), endurance runs (even worse), and recovery runs. It's a good thing I've decided to quit.

We walk in little clusters out to the track. Calvin's next to me. He's quiet and maybe still a little unsure but seems more confident than yesterday. That makes one of us, I guess. Kendra gives me a friendly wave before jogging out ahead of me on the track.

Coach Mendoza asks us to divide up by ability. "There's no shame in knowing how fast you run compared to others. Cross-country is a team sport, but it's also very individualized. I want our team to do well. But sometimes our team can have a bad day and yet we still have half a dozen runners who get PRs and so it's something to celebrate."

I nod, thankful for Uncle Jim's explanation last night. A PR, it turns out, is a "personal record."

"So I want you to decide if you're a fast runner, a decent runner, or a new and probably slower runner." This is a no-brainer for me. I head toward the turtles in the back.

While he talks, I notice that the football team is

practicing in the middle of the track. Great. I get to run in front of some of the biggest jocks in the school.

Kendra appears at my side. She's doing a little stationary jog to keep her legs warm. Sweat trickles down her dark-skinned cheeks.

"You ready, B.?"

It's a good question. Am I ready? My legs are jittery. My stomach's in knots. I feel as if I could puke. And I'm wishing I'd never seen that flyer in the library.

"Yeah, I'm ready." I swallow a burp.

"You'll be great." She grins and heads toward the middle group.

Across the football field is the bench where P. G. and I used to wait last year for my dad to come pick us both up. Seeing that bench gives me a hollow feeling in the pit of my stomach. Won't he be glad when I tell him I've quit. Maybe then we can hang out together again.

But wait. Is that what I really want? To give up and quit because P. G. says I can't do this?

Anger starts to build. I may be fat; but that doesn't mean I can't be on a team, be an athlete, be successful at something other than Honor Society. I'll give this run everything I have. I'll show him.

"Remember, guys," Coach is saying, "you don't have to kill yourself; but I don't want you sandbagging, either. Show me what you got. All right, runners, line up."

On Coach's whistle, the runners take off like

racehorses. I'm left alone, as usual, with the heaving of my chest and the pounding of my new shoes on the track. I try hard to block out the yells of the football coach and the grunts of the players as they smack into each other on the line of scrimmage. I notice when the first fast runner overtakes me. But I don't stop. I swipe at the sweat beading on my upper lip.

I think of P. G. and feel my resolve grow. It's crazy, really. P. G. got me through so many runs in PE. Laughing with me so we wouldn't feel the sting of embarrassment at being last. And now my anger at him is getting me through this run. I pound on, refusing to give him the satisfaction of being right.

The air is hot and heavy. I wonder if I'll make it the whole mile running. With every step, my sticky thighs rub each other until they actually feel raw. After the first lap Coach shouts, "Three minutes, forty-four seconds. Bennett, keep going!" I wonder again why I'm doing this. There are other ways to lose weight. Swimming. Weight lifting. Even football.

But then I think of P. G. again. *Kids like us, well, we don't run cross-country*. Fat kids, he means.

I start yelling at him in my head. *Who says fat kids can't run cross-country? Are you just going to use being fat as an excuse for the rest of your life? You want to end up like my dad, thrilled when he can feed himself applesauce and having to call a nurse when he has to pee?*

For the next three laps I silently call him every name I can think of—in both Spanish and English. I curse. I argue. Then I turn that final corner and see the finish line up ahead.

The rest of the team is done, sipping Gatorade from little cups. But as I stumble across the line, a good number of them turn. Someone shouts, "Good job, man!" Mark says, "Way to go!" Kendra claps me on the back and hands me a bottle of red Gatorade.

"You did it," she says. "One down."

I mumble, "One hundred more to go." She laughs.

My time is fourteen minutes and thirty-six seconds. The fastest time that day was six minutes flat.

But it's funny. Nobody is standing around bragging or anything. Nobody is looking at me as if I'm going to bring down the team. Everybody slurps up their sport drinks, chilling out.

"Man, it's hot," Mark comments to no one in particular.

"Got to HY-DRATE," some other kid says, mimicking Coach.

"Nice shoes, Bennett." I turn and see Calvin.

"Thanks, man." I admire them once again. "I can't believe how much these suckers cost, though."

"Okay, folks!" yells Coach Mendoza, waving his clipboard. "Before you go, make sure I've got your signed permission form. Make sure you've given me your phone number in case I have to reach you. You'll get your uniform on Friday. And our first meet is in two weeks at Tulane Hills. If any parents want to provide bananas or Gatorade for you guys, I'd be grateful. Great run today! Now get out of here!"

I start to walk toward the locker room with the other runners. But I hear Coach shout my name.

"Hey, Bennett! Can I talk to you a sec?"

Here it comes. The "you're just not cut out for this team" speech. I look down at my new shoes. And realize that I'm disappointed. That despite wanting to quit earlier, I don't want to now. I want to do this.

"Yeah, Coach." I swallow hard.

"Walk with me, will ya?" He slings a duffel bag over his shoulder and tucks his clipboard in it.

"How do you feel right now?" he asks.

"Hot. Tired. But all right, I guess." I keep my head down.

He stops. So I stop, too.

"You did good." His eyes are on me, honest and sincere. "You started and you finished. It wasn't easy for you. I saw that, and so did all the other runners. But you kept going and didn't stop."

I look up. Maybe I'm not about to be booted off the team.

"It's going to get harder, Bennett. I don't want to discourage you, but I want you to know what's coming. The sprints will take a toll on your knees and your shins, maybe your back. The hills are going to feel impossible. And the first two-mile run is going to feel like it never ends."

For someone who doesn't want to discourage me, he's doing a pretty good job.

"But I want you to know I'm behind you, okay? I think you can do this. When it gets hard, tell yourself it's nothing you can't handle. Running is only part physical. The rest is mental. Do you understand what I'm saying?"

"I think so, Coach."

He starts walking again. "See you tomorrow then, son."

"Yep, see you tomorrow," I say, and duck into the locker room.

And that's when I decide for sure: he *will* see me tomorrow. And next week and the week after. I started this. Now I have to finish.

Even if P. G. isn't behind me. No, make that *especially* if P. G. isn't behind me.

CHAPTER 21
In a Rut

Coach was right. It gets harder. A lot harder.

On Thursday we do hill repeats. After an "easy" mile warm-up, Coach leads us to this street north of our school that literally goes straight up. For two hundred meters we're supposed to run up that hill as fast as we possibly can. Then we'll jog down and do the whole thing again. And again.

He puts us in groups of four. I watch the first two groups go and actually think I'm going to be okay—it's not that long. Then my group is up.

Coach says, "Go!"

About a third of the way up the hill, it feels as if I'm not running anymore. In fact, I'm barely going anywhere at all. I'm moving my feet and my lungs are near exploding; but Mark, who is already at the top of the hill, isn't getting any closer. It takes Mark thirty-two seconds to run the two hundred meters. It takes me one and a half minutes.

He does five sets. I do two and a half before the earth starts spinning. I bolt to some nearby bushes and puke up the granola bar I ate right before practice.

Mark laughs as he walks toward me. "Everybody has to hurl once." He claps me on the back as I stand up and wipe my hand over my mouth. "But, dude, rule number one? Don't eat before practice!"

I smile weakly. Lesson learned.

For the rest of practice I have to sit on the curb. I swallow a whole lot of times. Ugh.

Coach says this is normal. Normal? What kind of crazy sport is this where it's normal to feel like you're going to die?

They don't have a uniform in my size, so Coach borrows a football jersey for me instead. I start to feel those old Fat Boy feelings surface as he hands me the gigantic jersey but shove them down quickly. I'm part of the team. As long I'm wearing blue and gold, who cares what the jersey looks like or what size it is, right?

Cross-country practice is a daily challenge. But it's actually not the part of my life I dread the most right now.

P. G. still isn't talking to me; and after three days of just me and my iPod, I've grown tired of eating in the library.

On Friday I learn that some of the guys from cross-country—Mark and a kid named Bryce—sit at the end of the wall. Feeling bold (and desperate), I ask if I can join them. Without hesitating they welcome me in. It doesn't feel as comfortable as it did with P. G., but at least it's better than staring at the librarian.

I worry that Luis might find me in my new eating location. Then all the cross-country kids will hear him call me Fat Boy. For that whole first lunch, I can barely talk. I keep looking around for Luis, waiting for him to pounce.

The one thing that's kept me going is knowing that I get to hang out with Taylor that night. I half expect her to text me and tell me that she's sorry but she has to cancel or something. The only message I get from her, though, says, "Hope you like Monopoly." Believe me, a part of me is superexcited to spend the evening with Taylor and her friend, but there's a big part of me that feels like hurling every time I think about it.

To top it off, my dad's in a rut as well.

On Friday afternoon I'm running a few minutes late. I rush into my dad's room, out of breath, and find Jameel waiting for me.

"Hey, Bennett," he says casually. "I'm glad you got here before your dad. I want to talk to you about something."

My heart sinks. This can't be good.

"So here's the thing," Jameel says, sitting on my dad's bed and looking straight at me. "I'm pushing your dad pretty hard right now. It's tough and it's painful. Some days he wants to give up."

Jameel smiles. "So if you can help him out, that'd be great. Give him a little pep talk. He listens to you."

Jameel heads out a few minutes later.

I walk over to the window and look down on the courtyard. If my dad doesn't keep pushing, we'll lose the insurance money. Jameel probably knows that, too. Which is why he wants me to motivate my dad. I blow out a big breath of air.

Then I hear the nurse push my dad into the room.

I spin around and paste a huge smile on my face. "Hey, Dad. How's it going?"

He glares at me.

"I talked to Aunt Molly yesterday. She's going to take a few days off in October and drive down to see us. I told her to bring some of Uncle Mike's baklava. But not too much, since the Robinson men are in training." I pat my stomach.

Another glare.

"How's your physical therapy coming along? Take a step or two yet?"

My dad shoots me a dirty look and slurs, "No. It's hard."

"It's going to be hard, Dad. You knew that."

My dad shakes his head. He won't look me in the eye.

"You can't give up, Dad." I kneel in front of him. "You've got to push through this. How can we ever go back to our house and the way things were before if you don't learn how to walk and talk?"

"You . . . don't . . . understand." He glares at me, resentful. Tired.

That's it. Something snaps.

"I don't understand?" I yell, standing up, leaning over

him. "You think I don't understand? I'll tell you what I *do* understand. I understand what it's like to try to run up a hill as fast as I can; but no matter how fast I run, I'm still the slowest kid by a mile! I have to go puke in the bushes—the poor, fat kid who can't hack it. I understand what it feels like to want to give up, Dad! Especially when my best friend has bailed on me because . . . well, I don't exactly know why, which makes it even more frustrating!"

My dad looks surprised.

"But I haven't given up, Dad! And I don't plan to! And I'd like to think I got that particular quality from you. Mom gave up, didn't she? Refused the chemo, refused the treatments. Just gave up."

I'm crying now. Jameel has come back into the room and is standing by the door. But he doesn't say anything.

"I know she did, Dad!" I sob. "That's why Aunt Laura was so mad that day! Mom gave up, and you let her! Well, I won't let you! DO YOU HEAR ME? I won't let you!"

I turn and bolt from his room, run down the hall and out the front doors. I collapse onto one of the benches that line the entrance walkway and cover my face with my hands.

What did I just do? Some great motivator I am, huh?

Everything from the past week comes bubbling up. I lose it. Sobs rack my body.

I feel someone sit next to me but don't bother to look up. I've been called Fat Boy, given a football jersey because I can't squeeze into a normal uniform, lost my best friend, and have a father who can't blow his own nose. Who cares if someone sees me crying right now?

After I've cried every tear I've got, I stop, wipe my nose on my sleeve, and turn.

Jameel is sitting next to me, casually, his arms resting wide-open along the back of the bench.

"Pretty sad, huh?" I laugh, wiping my cheeks with the backs of my hands. "A thirteen-year-old boy throwing a tantrum and then running out the door. Real mature."

"Actually," he says, not looking at me, "I think you probably should have done that a while ago."

"So they could call me a nutcase and lock me up?" It's a lame attempt at humor.

"No. So you could get it out of your system and realize you don't have to be Superman. Your mom's dead. Your dad had a stroke and is nowhere near being back to his old self. You're living with an aunt who seems okay but isn't your mom, and that sucks. You've got insurance idiots breathing down your neck—not to mention putting pressure on your dad. Sounds as if you might be having some issues with your best friend. And you're scared to death that if you don't lose weight yourself, you're going to end up like your dad. So you're pushing yourself beyond all limits; and if you're not careful, you're going to crack."

"I think I just did."

Jameel laughs, bumps his shoulder to mine.

"Kid." He smirks. "I've seen stronger people crack for a lot less. Look, Bennett, you're doing great, okay? In fact, you're doing amazing. Cut yourself some slack. You're losing weight. . . ."

"Really?" I look down at my bulging belly. "You think so?"

"Hello? Bennett? Anyone home?" Jameel looks at me as if I'm crazy. "Check out a mirror or a scale once in a while, dude. Those pants are about to fall off your skinny butt."

Now that he mentions it, they are pretty loose. And my T-shirt feels bigger. Roomier. Maybe I *should* look in a mirror. It's just that for so long, mirrors told me what I already knew.

"Your dad's going to be fine. I probably shouldn't have told you he was struggling, but I thought maybe you could offer a little encouragement. You being the athlete now and all, you might know how to motivate someone. I didn't know you were gonna go ballistic on me. Jeez!" He shakes his head in mock disgust.

"Yeah, I was kind of harsh, huh?"

"Well, I do think you might have shaken him out of his pity party."

I grin. "Make that a pity party for two, I guess."

"Bennett." His eyes grow serious. "That stuff about your mom. That was pretty heavy. Your dad didn't 'let' your mom die. He misses her every day of his life. I know, because I'm spending just about every day with him right now."

My throat tightens. Thinking about my mom, I'm

ready to start bawling all over again.

Man, if my mom were here right now, everything would be so much easier. But she chose to give up. I've always wondered how she could make that choice when she had a five-year-old son.

I sit there silently for a while. Jameel stays where he is, and I look out over the front lawn.

"Jameel?"

"Yo."

"Thanks."

"No problem, Bennett." He claps my back and goes inside. A few minutes later, I follow him.

My dad is still sitting in the same chair when I get back to his room. He's looking out the window but swings his head toward me when I come in. I sit across from him and look down at my hands. We're both silent for a while.

"Ben . . . nett." I look up. "I'm . . . not . . . quitting."

"I know, Dad." I swallow the lump that's forming in my throat. "I'm sorry. You didn't deserve all that. You're not a quitter." The tears start rolling again. I let them.

I see my dad suck in air. "Your mom . . . knew . . . she couldn't . . . beat . . . cancer." Each word is such an effort.

"I know, Dad. You don't have to . . ."

He holds up his hand. I shut up.

"She chose . . . to die with dignity . . . instead of . . . get beat down . . . by treatments. . . . They wouldn't have . . . worked. . . . It hurt her . . . to leave you." He closes his eyes, totally wiped out.

I feel the tears pouring down my cheeks. I let them come. I don't even wipe them away.

This is something I've needed to hear for eight years. Why have we never talked about this before?

I think back to the few memories I have of my mom. Walking me to the park, coloring endless numbers of pictures with me. Maybe she didn't just give up. Maybe she really did choose to make the most out of the time she had with me.

"Dad? We'll get through this, right?" My voice, barely audible, cracks.

"Yes," my dad says clearly. "Yes, we will."

"It's pretty hard." I swallow. "Right now, it's just hard."

"I . . . know." He slowly lifts his hand and reaches it out toward me. I grab it. With more strength than I thought he had, he squeezes my hand. I smile at him and squeeze back.

"We're quite a pair, aren't we?" I chuckle. "An overweight kid trying to run and a crippled guy trying to get uncrippled."

He smiles and kind of coughs, which I think is a laugh.

"Not . . . a . . . pair," he says. "A team."

"A team." I squeeze his hand again.

That makes two teams for me. Even without P. G. I'm stepping up to the plate more than I ever have before. Now, if I could just get a base hit.

CHAPTER 22
"Date" Night

It's Friday night. My night with Taylor and her neighbor. I'm supposed to be at Taylor's house by six thirty. At five thirty I'm in my room, panicking. No, more like hyperventilating.

What do you wear when the girl of your dreams asks you to come help her "baby-sit" a girl with cerebral palsy? I throw on a white T-shirt and jeans. The jeans are definitely loose, but I have no belt. Oh, well. They're cool that way, right? All baggy and hanging halfway down my butt? I just won't bend over is all.

Aunt Laura gets me to Taylor's house at six thirty on the button. She thinks it's "adorable" that I'm doing this. So adorable, in fact, that she even rescheduled her dinner plans so she could drop me off.

Unfortunately, she is excited enough about my "date" that she insists on walking me to Taylor's front door. I have a bad feeling about this. I'm very much wishing I had asked Uncle Jim to take me.

"Bennett," she says under her breath as we walk up to the door. "You remember to be a gentlemen, all right? Pull out her chair. Hold the door open for her. Offer to get her something to drink."

I roll my eyes. "Got it, Aunt Laura." My palms are sweaty. I really hope I don't have to shake her father's hand.

Aunt Laura swallows and looks at me uncomfortably. "I don't have to lecture you about . . . well, you know . . . being around a girl and . . ."

Good God! Could this get any more awkward?

"No, Aunt Laura. I'm all set on that stuff. Really."

I'm hugely grateful when Taylor answers the door seconds after I knock.

"Bennett!" She smiles and opens the door wide for me to come in. "I'm so glad you could come!"

"Yeah." I try to talk over the pounding of my heart. "Uh, me, too."

"I'm Bennett's Aunt Laura." My aunt extends her hand, all businesslike.

Taylor shakes it, and I can tell she's trying not to grin. I've told her a little about my aunt.

"Your parents are home, I imagine." My aunt cranes her neck to look past Taylor into the house.

"Yes, of course," Taylor says. "My mom is, anyway.

Bennett and I are gonna hang out with Maddy until about nine, when her mom is supposed to be back. My mom will drive him home after that, if that's okay."

"Yes, that's just fine." My aunt looks over at me one more time as if she's forgotten a whole bunch of advice she still wants to give me. Then she kind of sighs, says good-bye, and hurries back to her car.

Once Taylor closes the door behind us, she turns to me and puts her hand to her mouth.

"No way, Bennett! She's exactly like you said!" She laughs. "But you're lucky, at least, that she cares about you. It could be worse."

Yeah, I think. *She could be my real mom*. I shiver.

After saying a quick hello to Taylor's mom, I follow Taylor through the kitchen to the family room. There, on the couch, sits a very pretty girl in jeans and a T-shirt. She looks younger than us and has straight blond hair pulled back with a pink bow. Her head tilts to the right in a slightly awkward way. She's shaking a little bit.

"Hey, Maddy." Taylor nods at the girl. "This is the guy I was telling you about. Bennett."

Maddy smiles at me, though her smile is lopsided and her tremors seem to increase for a second.

"Hey, Bennett," she says. Her tongue gets kind of in the way on "Bennett," so it comes out slushy. She sounds a little like my dad.

"Hey, Maddy. Nice to meet you."

She grins. Something about this girl instantly puts me at ease.

"So, folks," Taylor says, clapping her hands, "here's the plan. Maddy loves Monopoly; and though she usually kicks my butt, I have agreed that we will play with her. Let me go grab a couple of sodas and some popcorn, and we'll get this party started. Sound okay, Bennett?"

"Great," I say. "But if you don't mind, I'll stick with water to drink."

Taylor pauses for the tiniest fraction of a second, then says easily, "Sure," and disappears into the kitchen.

I take a seat across from Maddy.

"So, how long have you known Taylor?"

"About five years." Maddy's head twitches. Her right arm is stiff and sort of jerky. With all the time I've spent with my dad lately, I mostly don't even notice.

"Cool," I say. "She says you really like baseball. Dodgers fan?"

She grins wickedly. "Padres."

I make a big show of pretending to be disgusted. "I can't believe it! Taylor expects me to hang out with a Padres fan? No can do."

Maddy laughs. "Probably best if you leave now. I'd have to rub it in that we won eleven of the fourteen games we played you this season."

I shake my head and cover my heart. "And Taylor has spoken so highly of you. I figured she'd have friends who are smarter than to root for the Padres!"

Maddy is laughing when Taylor walks back in with the popcorn and drinks. I notice Taylor's eyes light up when she sees us.

"What's going on in here?" she asks. "I've only been gone like, what? Two minutes?"

"You didn't tell me she was a Padres fan, Tay." I stop. The nickname rolled off my tongue so easily, but I look at her for any sign of a negative reaction.

Instead she hands me my water and grins. "Um, yeah, it's her one fault. But I promise, other than that she's perfect."

I shake my head and grumble, "Pretty big fault, if you ask me."

We choose our game pieces for Monopoly and within fifteen minutes are battling fiercely for properties. Taylor's right; Maddy is wicked good at this game. After an hour or so, she's kicking both of our butts.

As Maddy gets tired, her movements become jerkier. I notice Taylor has to help her move her game piece around the board a few times. Once, after rolling the dice, Maddy lets them go too soon and they fly across the room.

Taylor handles it like a pro. She raises her eyebrows at Maddy. "That's a new trick, girlfriend. Trying to get me to look away so you can steal my money. Bennett, keep an eye on my stuff while I go get the dice. She can't be trusted." She looks at Maddy pointedly, and Maddy dissolves into giggles.

My heart fills with respect and admiration for Taylor. And, okay, maybe a little more than that. Not only is she most definitely the kindest girl I know, but she also looks really good in her jeans as she bends to get those dice!

By eight forty-five when Maddy's mom shows up, I'm nearly bankrupt, and Taylor isn't doing much better.

"Thank God!" Taylor sighs when Maddy's mom walks into the room followed by Taylor's mom. "Bennett and I were about to lose the shirts on our backs. This girl is ruthless!"

Maddy grins happily, but I can see in her eyes that she's wiped out. She looks like my dad after a tough day of physical therapy.

"Not to mention a Padres fan," I mutter.

Maddy's mom laughs. "She doesn't get that from me, I promise you. I'm a Dodgers fan from way back. I think she started rooting for those stupid Padres just to irritate her dad and me."

"Well, there's hope then," I say. "At least someone in the family is sane."

We all laugh. Maddy's mom comes over to help her daughter to her feet. Maddy's pretty wobbly, and her right arm is bopping all over the place.

"Thanks, Taylor and Bennett," Maddy's mom says. "I'm sure she had a good time. More fun than coming to my bunco game."

Maddy rolls her eyes. "Yeah, thanks. You saved me

from two hours of gossip and every kind of salad that can possibly be made."

"It was fun," I say. "But next time we play Scrabble or something, okay? Unless you're like the national champion of that game, too?"

"Deal." Maddy limps unsteadily toward the door with her mom supporting her under her armpits.

Taylor's mom leaves to walk them out, and it's just me and Taylor in the room. I start cleaning up the game. It's suddenly awkward for the first time all night.

"This was fun," I say. "Thanks for inviting me."

Taylor hands me a wad of money to put back in the box.

"I'm, um, glad you came." She doesn't meet my eyes. I'm worried, then, that I did something wrong.

"You were right about Maddy. She's a really cool kid."

"Yeah, she doesn't let the fact that she can't always control her movements get her down."

I put the lid on the box.

"Seriously, Taylor." I stop and dare to look at her straight in the eyes. "It's really cool that you treat her like everyone else. It was so easy to just relax and hang out, you know?"

"You, too, Bennett." She smiles, and my heart somersaults. "I could tell you were comfortable with her. Thanks. I mean it." She reaches over and squeezes my hand. Miraculously, my hand isn't sweaty. I squeeze back. And even though she lets go quickly, I can feel the softness of her hand and the warmth of it long after.

On the car ride to Aunt Laura's house, a popular song comes on and Taylor's mom turns up the radio really loud. Taylor and I sing as loudly as we can. By the time I hop out of the car, I feel like I'm walking on air.

Nothing can spoil this night. Absolutely nothing.

CHAPTER 23
Run. Eat. Sleep. Repeat.

For the next week it takes all my energy to make it through each day. Survive school. Avoid Luis. Avoid P. G. Not puke at cross-country practice. Limp in to visit with my dad. Smile through the visit, encourage him to keep trying, trying, trying. Then hurry through homework, fall into bed, and repeat.

I'm very aware of the passage of time, though; each day brings us closer to that twenty-one-day deadline when the co-payment on the insurance kicks in. Uncle Jim hasn't said a word to me about it; neither has Aunt Laura. But no FOR SALE sign has gone up in front of our house yet, either. I know, because I made Uncle Jim take me there one afternoon.

By the following Sunday I want to dive into a bowl of Doritos and not come out. For the first time ever I'm grateful that my aunt doesn't keep junk food around the house. I would have gained back every pound I've lost.

Wednesday is the deadline for that idiot insurance company, which means I desperately need to hit the Lotto jackpot or raise fifteen grand to help my dad. Not gonna happen any time soon.

I've tried to get up the nerve to talk about it with my aunt, but each time I bailed out. What if she says we have to sell my house? I need to have a good argument prepared or another alternative, and I don't have either one yet.

To top it off, the first cross-country meet is Tuesday afternoon—just two days from now. No way am I ready.

And I'm still getting zip, zero, nada from P. G., even though I sent him a text message yesterday asking him to give me a call. I could really use his good-humored, straight-shooting wisdom. I'm willing to let bygones be bygones.

Today I tried calling his cell but got his voice mail— "P. G. Message. Beep." So I guess he's ignoring me. I think about calling his house but can't stomach Mrs. Gomez telling me awkwardly that P. G. isn't home when we both know he is. There's nothing I can do; and, well, it sucks.

Just like everything else in my life at the moment.

Josh promised to run with me this morning, but wildfires broke out in several places around Southern California on Saturday. Today the Santa Ana winds are howling out of the north, pushing along the flames. The sky is turning a murky gray, and ash is raining down on everything. The air quality—not healthy on a good day— goes from bad to "stay indoors."

At breakfast on Sunday my aunt suggests I visit my uncle's office, which has every piece of workout equipment known to mankind, including a treadmill. But I know who will be using the equipment in that private little gym: top-notch athletes working themselves back into shape after injuries. The thought of trudging along next to them doesn't sound fun.

So I spend Sunday with my dad, watching football. He's speaking more clearly now. And Jameel told me he can drink by himself (through a straw) and eat on his own as long as it's nothing that he has to cut, like steak, or balance on his fork, like peas.

Yeah, steak and peas. Real complicated, huh?

He still can't walk on his own. And his left side hangs limp for the most part. It worries me, you know? That he's not doing enough, improving quickly enough. That some guy in a tie behind a desk somewhere is going to read his file and say, "Nope, send him home. We're not funding this guy's vacation anymore." I don't know what we'd do then. I truly have no clue.

By Monday afternoon the winds have died down and the fires are somewhat contained, but the air is still pretty bad. Coach Mendoza decides not to let us run.

"With the race being tomorrow, we would have gone

easy today, anyway." I look down at my poor legs. This is probably the first day in two weeks they haven't ached. Another day off sounds okay to them.

Coach uses the practice time to explain to us newbies how a meet is scored.

"The team that wins each race is the one that has the lowest score for the first five runners of that team. For example, if Mark comes in first in his race, we get one point. If Bryce then comes in fourth, we now have five points. If our next three runners come in seventh, eighth, and ninth, that's twenty-four more points, for a total of twenty-nine. If that's the lowest score of the three schools, then we win that race. The overall winner is the school that has the lowest points total for all four races. Got it?"

I listen to everything Coach says from the top row of the metal bleachers where I sit with Mark and Bryce, but I know it doesn't really apply to me. I won't be anywhere near the front of the pack, and I definitely won't score for my team.

"Finally," Coach says, setting down his clipboard on the bleachers, "I have one big mission for you tonight."

Mark mutters, "Here it comes."

Coach, a smile playing around his lips, says, "I want you all peeing clear."

The kid next to me snorts. "Seriously? I gotta check out my pee?"

"You need to drink so much water between now and tomorrow's race that your urine looks like water and doesn't have much yellow to it. Plus, I want you eating a healthy dinner tonight: pasta, some protein, a vegetable." He looks down at his clipboard. "That's it for me. Hit the locker room, folks."

Everybody heads toward the locker rooms, chatting and laughing in small groups.

Mark punches my shoulder as he jogs past. "You ready for tomorrow, B.?"

I bob my chin once and grin.

The excitement of the team is contagious. Even Calvin looks pumped. But inside, I'm nervous. I don't want to let anyone down. I don't want to let myself down, either. That means I have to push harder than I have before, and I've already been pushing pretty hard.

With it being so hot and smoky outside, I figure I'll head to the library for twenty minutes to do some reading before Aunt Laura picks me up. I find an empty table and pull out the John Wooden book. It doesn't take long till I'm engrossed in the coach's stories.

Something pings the back of my head.

"Ha-ha! Fat Boy's here! I've missed you at lunch lately, Fat Boy."

Luis swings into a chair on the opposite side of the table, while his sidekicks—these two kids who follow him everywhere like bodyguards—stand on either side.

Great. What now?

But I'm consciously aware that it's not fear creeping into my chest. Not even dread, really. What I mostly feel right now is acceptance. Acceptance that this is the way things will always be for me. And that scares me more than anything.

I force myself to sit up straighter and look him in the eye. "Listen, man, I'm trying to read while I wait for my ride. Can't you just leave me alone for once?" I hope I sound firm, not whiny.

"Listen, man," Luis mimics. Then he turns fake sad eyes on me. "I thought we were getting close. You know, sharing lunch and all. And then you go and leave me. I'm hurt, man, really hurt! Your buddy still eats there, you know. You guys have a falling out or something? Fight over a chocolate bar?"

My eyes widen. P. G. still eats there? He wasn't there that one day I checked. But I guess I haven't come back since then. What if he was just late that day? What if he thinks *I* was the one who bailed?

Luis reaches over and rips the book from my hand. He looks at the cover. "Fat Boy's reading about sports, huh? Pretty dumb choice for someone who can't even do a sit-up." And in one quick motion he knocks over the water bottle I had sitting on the table and drops my book in the spreading puddle.

Then he stands up. "See ya, Fat Boy." He strides off,

laughing, his friends trailing behind.

I grab my soggy book, wipe it off on my shirt, and hurry out of the library.

Outside, squinting in the bright sunlight, I falter for a second.

Could I have stopped him? Called for the librarian? Stood up immediately to leave? Grabbed him as he started to walk off and slugged him? P. G. challenged me to fight back. I realize now that I don't even know how.

Thinking about P. G. makes my stomach feel heavy. Just one of about a million things that does that these days.

CHAPTER 24
When the Gun Goes Off . . . Run!

On Tuesday I wear my blue-and-yellow football jersey to school—as an official cross-country runner. Of course, I'm asked at least fourteen times what position I play on the football team. When I tell people I'm on the cross-country team, their eyes widen.

It feels kind of good.

P. G. won't look at me in science. I can't decide if I'm pissed off by that or just sad. Taylor, however, tells me I look great and wishes me good luck.

Tulane Hills sits on a nice, flat piece of land. I want to kiss that sweet, level ground. My team gathers under a lonely palm tree about fifty feet from the start-finish line. Besides Tulane, our other competitor today is Palm Grove Junior High. Their small group of green jerseys huddles to our left. They have about fifteen kids total, which means they don't even have enough runners for all four races.

"No sixth graders." Mark nods in their direction when

he sees me looking. "They'll only run the last two races."

Mark, Bryce, and I sit in a huddle and work on homework before it's time for us to warm up. Calvin sits nearby, munching on a banana and nervously tapping his pencil on his textbook.

Mark reaches over and grabs it. "Dude! Enough with the drums already!"

"Sorry," Calvin mumbles. Poor kid is going to have an ulcer by the time he starts his first race.

About fifteen minutes later, Coach gathers us in a tight circle. He orders us to do a short warm-up lap around the soccer field. Mark and Kendra lead us through some fast stretches. Then it's time for the first race: the sixth graders.

At the loud gun blast, the sixth-grade runners take off as one big pack; but miraculously, no one falls and gets trampled. I find that I'm yelling "Go! Go! Go!" to the whole crowd of them. They make the first turn on the course, and the pack starts to thin out, with the fastest runners pulling out in front and others starting to fall back. Truman does well, with three of our sixth graders crossing the finish line before the first Tulane Hills runner gets there.

The seventh-and-eighth-grades girls' race starts almost immediately. With three schools in this race, there are more runners, and they look faster. After the first mile we have only two girls in the top ten. Coach hollers to every runner who comes by.

"Kendra, catch one! Use your arms, girl!"

"Shanice, shorten your stride. You can pass her now; come on!"

"Move, Emily! That's it. Steady pace until the end."

As the last girls run by on that first lap, I walk with my six teammates to get my label and head to the start line. My heart speeds up. This has *plate time* written all over it.

"Remember, guys." Mark pulls us into a tight huddle. "Nobody jumps out too fast. Keep it steady for that first lap. Save the real gas for the last half mile, when you know what you've got left. We can do this."

Real gas. Right. I don't think my rumbling stomach is what he's referring to.

We jog in place and stretch, waiting for the girls to finish. I notice a small kid waving from the first bend in the course. I squint. Josh!

Knowing he's here is both reassuring and scary.

I wave back and notice my aunt Laura standing not far from him, in the same designer sweats she wore to the hospital on the day of my dad's stroke.

It's funny. I've lived with my aunt for a whole month now. And some days I can tolerate her. Other days I have to grit my teeth or avoid her completely.

And yet she's here. To cheer me on, I guess. I could dismiss it and say that Josh made her come, but I know down deep in my heart that's not true. She came because she wants me to do well. Maybe for her own satisfaction.

But she's still here.

Unlike my dad.

I close my eyes and picture him in his wheelchair, the left side of his mouth sagging and limp. What would all these kids say if they could see my dad? I suddenly realize that I don't *want* him here. I don't want Mark and Bryce, Kendra and Calvin to see my fat dad who can't talk, who can't always wipe the drool from his chin. And that makes me feel rotten.

The girls' race is over, so we line up. Mark and Bryce, our best runners, are in front, their toes on the start line. Predictably, I'm in the back. A lady with a megaphone comes over.

"You'll start with the gun. No pushing. Stay on the course at all times. If you run into any trouble, stay where you are and one of our course volunteers will find you. No jewelry or watches. Tuck in your shirts! Good luck, runners!"

There are probably thirty of us. Some of the kids in front look like they can probably run really fast.

"Hey, Bennett." I turn. It's Mark.

"Good luck, and have fun. First time is always pretty cool." He grins. Then he's back to focusing on the course ahead, crouching and leaning forward like Coach taught us to do.

The gun goes off, and we start running. I feel like a Pepsi bottle that's been shaken up. But I've been warned. I keep my cool and force my feet to move forward, to find a rhythm. I hear Mark and Bryce talking to our guys in the front of the pack.

"Find your pace! Settle in!"

"It's your race! Don't let them get in your head!"

The lead runners are pulling away quickly.

I hear someone shout, "Bennett, you got this!"

I don't look up. I tune out and focus on my breathing. *Breathe, Bennett. Breathe.*

It's hot. My legs are heavy. Two miles seems endless. Two yards seems endless.

Out of the corner of my eye, I see Aunt Laura snapping pictures. I'm not sure I'll ever want to see them. I probably resemble a hippopotamus in running shoes. Nice running shoes, though.

Breathe. In-two-three. Out-two-three. Sweat beads on my upper lip. I lick it away.

With the crowd behind me and the pack of runners stretching way ahead of me, adrenaline is fading fast. Putting one foot in front of the other gets tough. Still, I keep running.

There's only one other runner who is anywhere close to me. He's from Tulane Hills. He isn't as heavy as me, but he runs with a limp. He stays about ten paces in front of me. I make it my goal not to fall too far back.

Breathing is the hardest. It's so hot. The air feels thicker than usual. It could be leftover ash fluttering around from the fires. Or it could be my imagination.

But I'm having trouble sucking in enough air with each breath. I try to do the "in-two-three" and "out-two-three" thing in my head. Uncle Jim taught me this strategy about a week ago. Quickly, though, it becomes "In-two, out-two," which dissolves into a rapid "In-out." I'm struggling.

So I start talking. Not out loud—I'm not that dorky. But to myself.

You got this, man, I tell myself. *This is a few minutes of pain for a big payoff. You can't give up. People are watching you. They're cheering for you. You going to let them down? Don't let guys like Luis win. You are not Fat Boy. You're a runner. So keep running.*

I set little goals for myself.

Make it to that tree up there. And then when I get to the tree, I think, *Now get to the end of that fence.* I'm still only about ten paces behind the limping boy. And I'm still running.

I'm almost to the end of the first lap. I turn the corner around an equipment building, and a miracle happens. I pass someone. A boy with a green Palm Grove uniform is walking and clutching his side. As I pass him, I gasp, "You okay, man?"

He nods. "Side ache."

"Sorry," I say, but inside I can barely contain my joy. *I'm not last!*

I hear cheers as I approach the end of the first mile. People line both sides of the course, shouting and clapping. As I run by, Josh is whooping with one fist in the air. He runs along the edge of the course with me, screaming, "Go, Bennett! Go!"

I hear Coach yell, "All right, Bennett! Keep going! Use your arms!"

For a few moments my breath comes easier. My legs feel stronger. I might make it. I think I've even gained a pace or two on the limping kid.

Then the cheering behind me grows faint again. I realize I'm only halfway done. The pain in my legs from all my training is coming back. I still have a mile to go. For me, that's about twelve more minutes of running.

A lifetime.

The kid I passed earlier whizzes by, recovered from his side ache. And once again I'm last.

That's when I almost stop. I want to stop. I *need* to stop. Everything hurts. In a big way. My vision starts to cloud—from sweat, from dehydration. My head grows fuzzy. My brain clearly gives the order: *stop*. Apparently, my feet don't hear it, because they keep going.

Come on, just stop, I urge my feet. But they don't. It's like somebody has pressed the autopilot button. I just keep going.

I lift my head slightly when I see running shoes that aren't mine in my peripheral vision. I've caught up to the limping kid. I look over at him as I run. His face is red, really red. His eyes are half closed. It looks as if his right leg is really hurting him, so his steps are uneven. His breathing is raspy.

"You okay?" I ask, using up precious oxygen.

He nods, just barely. Keeps running. Keeps gasping. I'm impressed.

I, too, keep running.

I start to make deals with myself again. *Run another minute, and you can walk. Finish this race, and you can quit cross-country. Don't puke, and you can have an ice cream sundae later.* And over and over I keep telling myself that I am a runner, not a Fat Boy. I will make this last mile.

And somehow, I do. I round that equipment house for the last time. And there it is: the finish line.

It's crowded with people, all watching me and the limping kid as we slowly get closer. I want to shout for joy, but I have no energy. I push forward and hope I don't collapse before I cross that line.

I have only twenty feet to go when I find this tiny drop of energy. With a pitiful burst of speed, I cross the line inches ahead of the limping kid. Feeling light-headed, like I could puke any second, I manage to get over to the table and peel off my label. The man behind the table takes it and smiles.

"Nice job."

I don't know what time I finished in, and I don't care. I'm done.

Suddenly, I'm surrounded by people. My teammates crowd in. Hands clap me on the back, slapping my sweat-soaked shirt. I hear "Good job, man!" through the buzzing in my ears. Someone hands me a small Dixie cup of water. I try to drink it, but my hand is shaking and I spill a ton of it.

Coach grabs my shoulders and says, "You did it, Bennett! Now keep walking slowly, and all that mess in your head and your stomach will go away. I promise."

I want to sink onto the grass and never get back up. But I keep shuffling my feet forward, thankful for every breath that gets me closer to normal again. The buzzing in my ears fades, and my stomach doesn't feel like it's ready to unload anymore. Forget belly button stains: the sweat pours off me in waterfalls. I grab the bottom of my shirt, wiping the sweat from stinging my eyes as I somehow find my way to Aunt Laura and Josh.

"Bennett!" Josh screams, eyes shining. "You ran the whole thing! You ran two miles! You're awesome! I knew you could do it!"

I grin stupidly at his excitement. I'm so glad he's my cousin, so glad he's here.

"Let me get a picture of you, Bennett," Aunt Laura commands.

I sling my sweaty arm around Josh and try to smile. How gross do I look? But I'm a gross-looking *runner*, and that's cool.

"You did great, Bennett," Aunt Laura says. "Really great. Your dad's going to be extremely proud of you."

With all the runners in, Coach starts shouting orders

to clean up our trash, grab our backpacks, find our water bottles, get on the bus. I tell Aunt Laura and Josh I'll see them at the house and join my team.

My team. Walking to the bus, I remember how P. G. got so mad at me for saying that. I felt kind of embarrassed, because it hadn't really been accurate at the time.

Not anymore. Now, this *is* my team. I pulled my weight today . . . literally. I may not have affected the outcome of the meet, but I also didn't let anyone down, or embarrass anyone.

Yeah, I'm feeling good. I just wish I had a best friend to share it with.

CHAPTER 25
Counting Down the Days

September speeds up after that first cross-country meet.

And, believe me, nobody's paying more attention to the time than me. Each day that passes, I make an imaginary red X in a square, just like I did before my fifth birthday. But this time I'm not wishing the days away. I'm wishing they would slow down.

My dad needs every flippin' one of them.

Day 21 comes and goes, and no one says anything to me about it. Not Aunt Laura. Not Uncle Jim. Somehow this worries me even more. Several times I almost ask who's paying the co-payment for my dad, but I'm afraid of the answer. I wonder if my aunt and uncle are paying it and we'll have this huge debt when my dad gets out.

Dad is making incredible progress. If the insurance guys wanted results, they're getting them. He's speaking in full sentences now, though his words are slurred. The left side of his body still moves slower than his right. But Jameel has him using weights and weight machines. For one of the machines, Dad has to sit on a bench and lift a weighted bar with his legs. It looks tough, even for me. But my dad grimaces and grunts his way through it. And it's giving him back some muscle in his arms and legs.

He's also losing weight.

Jameel says that when he first saw my dad at the beginning of September, he weighed close to four hundred pounds.

"He's down to about three hundred and fifty now," Jameel tells me one day when I comment on my dad's slimmer face. "But he's lost fat and muscle both. What we want to do is build the muscle, continue to lose the fat, and teach your dad how to choose healthy foods so that the weight doesn't come back when you get home."

Dad's not the only one slimming down. It's official: I've dropped a full pant size. I'm no longer buying XXLs, but simply XLs. I've lost a chin. And I just *feel* better—less sloppy, less tired. I can get to the top of the stairs at Aunt Laura's house without gasping for air.

I know my weight loss must be noticeable, because yesterday afternoon Kiley actually paused before ducking into her room and acknowledged my presence long enough to say "Hey, you look sorta, like, okay in those jeans."

Yeah, I nearly choked up.

I owe a lot of my weight loss to cross-country. But I'm

still getting up on my own every morning at six thirty. Now I actually look forward to it. Some days I walk only a few miles. Other mornings I get up and run a little bit with Uncle Jim. Two miles is still a long run for me, but I'm getting better. Faster, too.

And then there's Coach Mendoza's training. Hills. Sprints. Intervals. Speed work. Conditioning. It comes by different names, but it all means the same thing: pain. My legs constantly ache. On the few (very few) days when he says "Today's an easy day," I cheer. That means we run on the track for about twenty minutes—and that now qualifies as "easy" to me.

Our second cross-country meet happens a few days after our first one. Even though I feel more prepared for it, I think my body's still recovering from the race earlier in the week. By the second mile, I feel as if I'm running through mud. My time is slower, but Coach Mendoza tells me not to be discouraged. He does, however, tell me to "ice" that night in the bathtub (not fun) and then take the weekend off to let my legs recover (thank God).

Despite my backward progress and the constant pain my legs are in, I'm more determined than ever to finish this season of cross-country. No matter what P. G. thinks, fat kids can be runners, too. Decent runners, even.

Plus, I'm really having a good time with Mark and Bryce. We have lunch together every day and text each other in the evenings. We're too busy with running to do much together outside of school, but they joke around with me at practice and make me feel like I'm one of the guys.

But I miss P. G. A lot. I know I have to do something about him soon. I just don't know what.

The following Tuesday we have our third cross-country meet. It's a flat course, and with my legs feeling rested, I get a PR.

Coach claps me on the back at the finish line and tells me we need to work on my "kick"—whatever the heck that means. I thought this was cross-country, not soccer.

That night, while I'm sitting at the kitchen table with bags of frozen peas on my aching knees, wondering why I took up this sport in the first place, Aunt Laura asks me about P. G. "Something happen between you guys?"

She's cooking dinner, a little later than normal because both Kiley and Josh had soccer games that didn't end until seven.

"Uh, no." I look down at my throbbing legs.

"How does P. G. feel about you running cross-country?"

I look up at her. How does she know? My dad would have said, "Where's P. G.? I miss the little twerp." And I would have muttered something about him being busy, and that would have been it.

I'm hesitant. "He hasn't been too excited about it, I guess."

"Really? Why do you think that is?" She doesn't look at me, just keeps stirring whatever she's stirring.

"I don't know," I say. And then, I guess because I have

no one else to talk to about it, I keep going. "Actually, he was a real jerk when I told him. He made some remark about fat kids like us not being able to run. And then he made fun of me because I said something about it being 'my' team. I don't get it. It's not that big a deal."

"Maybe to him it is."

"What do you mean? He's not the one out there sweating every day and busting his butt." Anger's rising fast in my throat.

"Exactly." Aunt Laura stirs the pan calmly. "Let me ask you this. If P. G. was the one running cross-country while you continued doing the things you've always done, how would you feel?"

"Well, I'd like to think I'd feel happy for him."

"Sure. And maybe you would. But wouldn't you be the teensiest bit worried, too?"

Maybe I'm dumb or something, but I'm not getting this. "Worried about what?"

She flips the stove off, takes the pan off the burner, and turns to look at me.

"Worried that he would change and you wouldn't. Worried that, at some point, he wouldn't be a fat kid anymore and you would. Worried that he'd have a new group of skinny, athletic friends—the kind who in the past made fun of kids like you. Come on, Bennett. P. G. is terrified he's going to lose you, or that you're going to change so much that he won't like you anymore or you won't like him. I'll bet right now he's madder than a hornet, thinking 'I knew Bennett would drop me like a hot potato once he got all his cool, athletic friends. I knew he would think he was too cool for me.' But inside, he's wishing you would call him, prove him wrong, show that you still *do* want to be his friend. That you *need* his friendship."

"But that's stupid." She has to be wrong. "Why should I have to prove to him that I *need* his friendship? I never had to do that before. We were just . . . friends. Why did it have to change?"

"Because *you* changed," she says quietly.

"No, I haven't . . ."

But then I stop.

I look down at myself. I'm still in my running shorts and shoes. And I know, seeing those frozen vegetables on my legs, that I have changed. I've lost weight, gained muscle. I eat better. But it's more than that. I've learned— no, RElearned—that the people you care about can be taken from you at any second. I've started to realize that I can do stuff that I thought I couldn't.

And if that happened to P. G., would I have worried? Would I have been jealous? Would I have tried to talk him out of joining the cross-country team?

If I'm being honest: yeah, maybe.

Aunt Laura starts grabbing plates for dinner and calls everyone to the kitchen. I take the two bags of peas and gingerly walk over to put them back in the freezer.

What if she's right? And then I get an even stranger thought:

Am I wrong about Aunt Laura?

Can I talk to my aunt about my dad's insurance dilemma? Do I have any other options, really?

"Plate time," I whisper to myself. Again.

God, I'm getting good at this.

CHAPTER 26
Love Notes and Side Cramps

I'm huddled over my literature book in English class, trying to stay awake. Volunteers are taking turns reading a story about migrant workers in Northern California. My mind wanders. Did I bring an extra Gatorade for the meet this afternoon? Charge my watch?

Bam!

Somebody kicks me. Startled, I bump the table with my knee. Its metal legs scrape loudly as they slide across the linoleum.

Mrs. Curtis glances in my direction. I quickly look back down at my book. When she finally turns away, I stare pointedly at Taylor and mouth, "What was that for?"

Smoothly, she slides a folded-up piece of paper across the table. Just as smoothly, I slide my textbook forward to cover it. Taylor goes back to reading as if nothing's happened.

Not since first grade have I been passed a note by a girl. And that was when Haley Scarlotta handed me a folded piece of paper that read "Please don't pick me on your team at recess today."

My mind spins with possibilities. Another game night with her neighbor? The title of another book she likes? A confession of her undying love for me? Hah!

With five minutes to go in the period, Mrs. Curtis finally cuts us a break. "Read the rest of the story for homework, ladies and gents. And be ready for a quiz tomorrow." We close our books, relieved.

Trying to be as cool as possible, I tuck my literature book in my backpack and hide the note in the palm of my hand. When there's enough chaos in the classroom, I unfold it.

> *Hi, Bennett,*
> *Good luck at your cross-country meet today.*
> *I hope you do well. Text me when you're*
> *done and let me know how it went.* ♥ *Taylor*

Okay, so it isn't a confession of love. But, holy crap! I look up and grin.

"Thanks."

"Well," she says, looking away and fingering the zipper on her backpack, "I mean it. Good luck. Break a leg or whatever you guys say before a race."

"Well, leg breaking isn't generally what we runners prefer to talk about."

She laughs, and it's like the sweet sound of birds in the first hours of morning. I know those hours well now. I know those birds, too.

The bell rings seconds later. We file out, me right behind her. In the hallway she turns and does this cute little wavy thing with her fingers, then disappears into the flow of students. I swear I have never seen a cuter girl in my life.

I look down at her note in my hand, and I can't stop smiling.

Until someone rips it from my hand.

Before I can grab the note back, Luis has it open and is scanning it.

He looks up at me, his eyes narrowed.

"'*Text me when you're done and let me know how it went,*'" he mocks. "Oh, how cute!"

I grab for the note and jam it into my pocket.

Luis is winding up. "Dude, don't tell me you think she actually likes you? Why would any girl like a fat kid like you?"

I start walking toward my next class. Luis falls in step next to me.

"She's probably trying to win a bet with all her friends. Pretend to like the Fat Boy for a month and see if he believes it. She shows your text messages to her friends to prove she's reeling you in. Sucker!" he sneers in my ear.

I stop walking. It takes a second, but he does, too.

"Why do you hate me so much, Luis?" I keep my tone even. Can't let him see me sweat.

Other kids are listening in. Luis takes half a step backward. His eyes widen. "I don't hate you. I don't even *care* about you."

"Then why do you have to mess with me? If you don't care about me, then why not just leave me alone?"

"Where's the fun in that?" He laughs. He walks a few steps backward. "You better get to class, Fat Boy, or you'll be tardy!"

My cheeks flush. He may not hate me, but I'm pretty close to hating him. I sigh and hurry to class.

The cross-country meet that afternoon—my fourth one of the season—turns out to really suck.

A horrible side cramp hits me after one mile. I try to push through it; but by the last half mile, I'm spent. I walk the rest of the course and only pick it up to a jog as I cross the finish line—a full minute behind the last of the other runners.

Riding home on the bus, Mark and Bryce offer sympathy about the side cramp, saying it happens to everyone.

"Yeah." I shake my head. "But does it make everyone come in last?"

"Listen, man," says Bryce. "Somebody has to come in

last. Today it was you. It happens. Shake it off."

"Coming from the guy who ran his two miles in what, like, twelve minutes?"

"Uh, eleven thirty-nine, to be exact." His eyes drop sheepishly from mine.

"Seriously, Bryce. That time is sick. Well done."

"I bet we took the meet." Mark tosses a small Snickers bar in his mouth. I stare longingly at it, then look away. "Guess we'll know tomorrow when Coach gives us the results."

"Wet," says Bryce, using his new word.

Bryce likes to invent new words for *cool* and try them out. He started using the word *wet* last week in place of *sick* and *sweet*. I still grin when he says it. It's better than his previous word of the week: *meaty*. Mark and I busted a gut laughing every time he said, "Meaty, dudes." After two days, Bryce wisely switched to *wet*. His ultimate goal is to see if he can get one of his words to catch on with the whole student body.

Shyeah, right.

• • •

That night I text Taylor that I'm pretty sure we won, but we won't know until Coach gets our official results back from the hosting school. I quickly explain the side cramp and the last-place finish.

She texts back that I should be proud of myself. And that she's planning to come to my next meet so she can cheer for me. Then she sends a goofy picture of herself with one finger held up and the message "Bennett's #1." It's so cute that I stare at it for about five minutes before making it my wallpaper.

A girl's picture as *my* wallpaper. Who would have guessed?

I'm dying to tell someone. But who? As cool as Bryce and Mark are, I don't know them well enough to share something this major. P. G. would have understood how cool this is for me. But then again, maybe not. Maybe it would have been just another example of how I've changed.

Anyway, I'm still disappointed I didn't run the whole two-mile course at the meet. So I promise myself I'll run two and a half in the morning. It means getting up at six fifteen, but sometimes you have to sacrifice to reach your goals, right?

Unfortunately, my alarm doesn't go off . . . probably because I forgot to hit the ALARM SET button. Aunt Laura wakes me at seven thirty. I know instantly that there's way too much light streaming in my window. My running plan is down the toilet. I have just enough time to shower and hop in the car, stuffing last night's homework in my folder as I close the car door.

I check my phone for messages, still irritated for being so stupid with the alarm, when Josh looks over at me.

"Hey, Bennett? You got practice today?"

"Yeah, but it's supposed to be a short one since we had a meet yesterday."

"Do you think maybe you'd have time this afternoon to look over this speech I wrote? I'm going for sixth-grade vice president on Friday."

"Uh, that's great, Josh." I'm looking at a new message from Taylor on my phone. It just says "C U in English." No hearts this time. Oh, well.

I turn to Josh. "I was hoping to get in a run after visiting my dad. Uh, maybe tomorrow?"

"Sure." He looks away but not before I see the hurt in his eyes.

Which royally irritates me. I have the sudden urge to scream at him, *You're not my brother, so quit acting like it!*

Kiley, meanwhile, won't shut up.

"So then Michael told Sarah who told Chloe that he thinks I have the prettiest smile in the whole class and seriously, Mom, I think he might ask me to the first dance next week so we need to go shopping . . ."

I close my eyes against the headache that is rapidly forming and lean my head against the window for the rest of the ride.

At school I hop out of the car quickly and slam the door, happy to be getting away from that whole family. Since I've missed breakfast, I head to the cafeteria.

There are about three kids in line with me, all with wrinkled T-shirts, mussed-up hair, and sleepy eyes. I grab a doughnut—yes, a *doughnut,* so sue me!—and hand the cashier my change. I scan the tables for an empty one so I can study for my history test while I eat. That's when I notice a familiar shape bunched in a corner of the cafeteria: P. G.

Other than in science class, I haven't seen P. G. for a few weeks now. He doesn't notice me; his head is down, and he has on headphones. He's paging with disinterest through some textbook.

Plate time, Bennett.

I take a deep breath and head over. P. G. looks up, startled, as I sit across from him. He eyes me suspiciously but cuts his music and pulls off the headphones.

"Hey," I say cautiously.

"Hey." He looks back down at his book. He isn't going to make this easy.

"I haven't seen you for a while."

"Maybe you haven't been looking. I been here." His tone is tense. He's still eyeing his book.

"P. G., come on. It's me. Bennett."

"Is it?" He looks up with glaring, angry eyes. "'Cause you don't look like the Bennett I know. Knew."

"Because I've lost a few pounds?" Irritation builds in my chest. "Because I wear running shoes now? Come on. That's dumb."

"You calling me dumb now, bro?" He slams his book closed. "I'll tell you what's dumb. You hanging with some stupid jocks. Trying to lose weight to impress a chick. Spending all your time practicing for a sport you ain't never gonna be good at."

"You've got it all wrong, P. G. What's dumb," I say, my voice rising, "is dropping your best friend because he doesn't want to end up in the hospital like his dad." I stand up. "*That's* what's dumb, P. G."

I grab my backpack and walk away, leaving my doughnut uneaten on the table. I'm not hungry anymore, anyway.

Aunt Laura was right. He's worried I've changed too much. But he won't even take the time to see that the changes I've made have nothing to do with our friendship. He won't listen!

It's not even first period, and this day already sucks. As I throw myself into my desk chair, I think, *Well, it can't possibly get any worse.*

Boy, am I wrong.

CHAPTER 27
Dodging Crap

The thing about bad days is this: they're never like kinda bad or half bad. Nope, they're usually all-out, totally crappy bad.

Science with P. G. is fifty minutes of dodging crap.

Ten minutes into class Mr. Greer tells everyone to partner up for a lab. There are three of us at our table since one girl is absent. As we dip our litmus strips in different liquids to figure out which are bases and which are acids, P. G. and I refuse to speak to each other. By the end of the period I have another headache from sniffing all the chemicals. Mostly, though, I'm exhausted from trying to avoid P. G.

In English I realize I forgot to read the rest of the story we were assigned. So when Mrs. Curtis announces a pop quiz, my heart drops into my stomach. I'm sunk. Taylor looks at me sympathetically but turns in her paper after about three minutes, leaving no doubt she read the stupid thing.

Then we're supposed to read silently while Mrs. Curtis corrects our quizzes. My stomach, empty from no breakfast, starts moaning and groaning so loudly that it's like a bullfrog belching. The kids around me keep glancing up. Even Taylor looks up once.

Jeez, people, I want to yell, *haven't you ever had an empty, growling stomach before?*

By noon my stomach is one rumbling black hole of hunger. I'm heading for Mark and Bryce when I realize I forgot my lunch in my hurry out the door. I have exactly fifty cents left over from breakfast, enough for a carton of milk.

"All I got is a peanut butter and jelly, but you're welcome to half of it," offers Bryce.

Gratefully, I reach for the tiny rectangle he holds out. "I'll get you back tomorrow, man."

"Dude, 'preciate the offer." Bryce wrinkles his nose. "But those wheat grass, turkey things your aunt makes aren't my idea of a lunch."

I laugh. "Yeah, me either."

I polish off the last bite of sandwich and bend over to stuff a book into my bag. That's when I hear it.

"Ha-ha! So this is where you've been hiding at lunch, eh?"

Without even looking up, I know. I feel my face drain of color. I've been dreading this moment for a while, but I can't say I'm surprised. I sigh in defeat and raise my head.

"Hey, Fat Boy!" Luis calls out gleefully. "These your new friends? Jocks, eh? Nice! Where's the other Fat Boy?"

Luis's sidekicks are with him, standing guard like always.

I glance at Mark and Bryce, who raise their eyebrows in confusion.

"Sorry, guys," I say. "I've tried to ignore him for weeks now, and he just won't go away."

"Go away?" Luis puts his hand to his heart, pretending to be hurt. "But, Fat Boy, I thought we were friends."

"Come on," I say to Mark and Bryce. "Let's go."

We start to gather our stuff.

Luis's tone changes. "Don't walk away from me, Fat Boy. Not when I'm talking to you."

Maybe it's the day I'm having. Maybe Mark and Bryce being there makes me brave. Or maybe I just really don't want to take his crap anymore.

"I am done talking to you," I say, and start walking away.

Luis jumps in my path. His friends back him up. He gets right in my face.

"Listen here, Fat Boy. You ain't nothing but a two-ton piece of crap. A cake-eating zero. You need to remember who you're talking to."

"I know exactly who I'm talking to." I refuse to back away. "I'm talking to the guy who whines that he can't run the mile in PE because he forgot his tennis shoes when really he's worried he might run it even slower than me. I'm talking to the guy who picks on people like me because he's afraid someone might find out what a loser he really is. I know who I'm talking to, Luis. And I'm done now." I try to brush past him and keep walking.

He grabs my arm hard to spin me around, but it's like a Chihuahua trying to manhandle a German shepherd. My feet stay planted. Awkwardly, he lets go of my arm and faces me again.

"Listen. You better watch your back. You just made an enemy. And once you're my enemy, you're always my enemy; you hear me? Watch. Your. Back."

With one last glare in my direction, he spins on his heel and struts off.

I can feel my pulse in my temples. I try to take slow and calming breaths.

Mark and Bryce move into my line of sight.

"What was that all about?" Mark asks incredulously. "You sure you want to mess with Luis Gonzalez? I've heard he's got a record! Like a real record, with the cops!"

Bryce nods. "Yeah, and didn't he, like, get caught stealing last year?"

I run a shaky hand through my hair.

"Dude!" Bryce says. "That was crazy! I've never seen anyone stand up to him before. You're like my idol! And that stuff about him not ever having PE shoes? That was so wet!"

"I don't know where it came from. I wasn't even thinking, I guess."

They walk with me for a few more minutes, reliving the encounter until the bell rings. I head off to class without them. Alone, in the halls, I have to wonder if I'll regret what just happened.

I'm now on the hit list of one of the scariest dudes in school.

But, man, I wish P. G. had been there.

CHAPTER 28
The Last Straw

A small Post-it note on my locker reads "I'm watching you, Fat Boy." I rip it off.

After PE I change into my running gear and go out to meet the rest of the cross-country team. Our fifth meet is next week—the last one before the finals—and it's at Meadowbrook Middle School. Josh and Kiley's school. Even though my cousins aren't on the cross-country team, it's still going to be weird to compete against them. I really hope I can do better than I did at the last race.

Coach has us skip our warm-up run, tells us to sit down on the bleachers. His eyes scan over us. They're very serious, missing their familiar sparkle. A few kids straggle in, and he snaps at them to hurry up. Mark looks at me, eyebrows raised. I shrug. Something's up. This isn't like Coach at all.

"Okay, folks." He drops his clipboard on the bleachers. "You're probably wondering what's going on, why I've started practice like this. Well, I've got some news that's going to affect the next meet, and I want you guys to hear it from me. I know how middle school is. Rumors fly, and things spread that aren't true."

Suddenly, I get a bad feeling in my stomach.

"Calvin's mom called me this morning. His grandfather passed away last night. The whole family will be flying to Virginia tomorrow to attend the funeral and spend time with family. That means he'll miss next week's meet."

Ah, man. My heart goes out to Calvin. Losing a family member is tough. Nobody knows that better than me.

The team starts mumbling things like "Poor Calvin" and "That sucks."

Coach holds up his hand. He's not done.

"About an hour after Calvin's mother called, Vindeep's mom called me."

Vindeep is a seventh grader, like Calvin, who usually places in the top ten, though closer to tenth than first. He's a nice kid, a little quiet.

"He had a seizure last night—no one is sure why—and is being hospitalized. He's been in and out of consciousness; and until they find out what's wrong with him, he won't be back at school. Or, obviously, running cross-country."

Wow. You don't think of your classmates having things like seizures. That's for old people or people who are really sick. Not guys who just ran a two-mile race with you only twenty-four hours ago.

Coach takes off his baseball cap, runs a hand through his thinning hair, and puts his cap back on. His face is tired and drawn. He looks up at us. In fact, it seems as if he looks right at *me*.

"For our team, it means that we have five guys running in the race next week. Mark, Bryce, Eduardo, Kaleem, and Bennett. That means all five of you guys score for us no matter what place you come in. That's a lot of pressure. But I want you to know we're all going to be encouraging you; and no matter what that final score is, we'll be cheering and proud of you."

I know then why it seems as if he's talking to me. My run matters this time. Where I place will determine whether we win or lose.

My first races were pressure enough—not wanting to let my team down, not wanting to come in so far last that I was the laughingstock of the meet.

But to be responsible for the outcome of the race?

A weight settles in on my shoulders. I've really only been running for about a month. And though I've been running pretty much daily, I'm still overweight. And let's be honest here: I'm not an athlete. Not by any stretch of the word.

Mark and Bryce could run their butts off, break records, place first and second. But if I come in last it jacks our score up so much we lose. And at Meadowbrook of all places! Aunt Laura and Uncle Jim are both coming. Josh. Kiley. Even Taylor.

LOSING IT

When I close my eyes, I can picture her so clearly. Her chestnut hair falling in her face when she's taking notes in English. Her silly smile that greets me every time I flip on my phone. I don't want her to see me fail, or watch me make my team lose.

It's all over. The charade is up. I'm the same old Bennett. The unknown middle school student who doesn't get involved in stuff. Who doesn't make waves or face down bullies.

Right now I want to walk home to my old house, flop on the couch with some Ruffles, and wait for my dad to come home so we can watch the Dodgers and eat burgers. That's easy. That's safe.

Being one of five guys who has to score? Not safe.

You've heard people say that their lives flashed before their eyes? Well, at that moment stuff starts coming at me like I'm flying through an asteroid field. I'm dodging deadly space rocks for all I'm worth.

Luis and his threats.

P. G. and his pissy attitude.

My dad and our money problems.

My aunt expecting me to be somebody I'm not.

My team needing me to perform.

And me—the fat kid pretending to be an athlete.

I can't do it anymore. I'm done. Tapped out.

Coach is telling everyone the official results of yesterday's meet. I don't hear what he says, but my time isn't something to care much about, anyway.

"Great job yesterday." He looks around. "Listen, next week's meet is the qualifier for the championship meet in a few weeks. We've done well so far. We have a good shot to get into the finals. Meadowbrook is currently tied with us, so how we do there will tell us whether we make it or not."

I'm sure someone has taken a bat to my abdomen. I've been sucker punched.

"We're a good team. No, a great team. Even short-handed, we can do well."

There's no secret at this point who he's talking about. Everybody on those benches knows who next week's meet is riding on. Most of them refuse to look at me.

"Let's do a quick jog around the fields here and call it a day, okay? We'll practice tomorrow."

"Even though it's Friday?" Kendra asks.

"Yep, even though it's Friday." Coach points to his left, signaling us to get running.

The team climbs down off the bleachers. Everyone is unusually quiet.

I don't move.

Mark looks back over his shoulder. "You coming, Bennett?"

"Yeah," I say. But I'm not.

Mark pauses for a second. Opens his mouth. Closes it. Then he shakes his head slightly and trots off behind the team.

Coach gathers his stuff and gets ready to follow. That's

when he looks up and notices me sitting there.

"You good, Bennett?" I know he's asking me about the meet.

I nod. But I'm not good. Not at all.

"I know this is probably a lot for you to take in. But you're capable of doing this, Bennett. I know it, and you know it."

And that's when I know he's wrong.

I stand up quickly. Instead of running after the team, I head for the locker room. It's like a voice in my head just keeps repeating, *Nope. Can't. Done. Stop. Quit. Over.*

I hear Coach call after me, but I don't care.

For the first time, running is getting me away from something. I know it won't help. I know it never works. But still, there I am. Running away.

CHAPTER 29
Want. Food.

Despite what I told Josh this morning in the car, I don't go to see my dad that night and I don't run.

"You okay, Bennett?" my aunt asks when I slide into the backseat of the car. Neither Josh nor Kiley are in their usual spots. But I'm too caught up in my own misery to ask where they are.

"Yeah," I mumble. "Headache."

"Here." She fumbles in her purse and passes back a bottle of Tylenol. "And drink some water. Did you forget your water bottle again? You have to drink when you run, Bennett. No wonder your head hurts! Most headaches are caused by dehydration, you know."

Or aunts who won't shut up.

I flip open the Tylenol, shake out one, and hand the bottle back to her. I stealthily drop the little round pill in my pocket.

She looks back at me in the rearview mirror.

"You sure it's just a headache?" She peers at me more closely.

"Yeah." I rub my temple for effect. "And I've got a big science test tomorrow. A lot to study tonight."

She drops me off before going to pick up Kiley and Josh. I let myself into the empty, quiet house.

For a second I don't move. I just stand in the entryway. My head actually is starting to hurt. I reach into my pocket for the Tylenol and go to the kitchen for some juice. But when I open the refrigerator door, there's half of a chocolate cake sitting on the top shelf.

I don't know why it's there. Aunt Laura almost never has sugary, fattening foods in the house. But she hosted a bunco game earlier this week, so I guess it's left over from that. It'll probably be thrown out at any minute.

I reach in and swipe my finger through the frosting. I close my eyes when the chocolate hits my tongue. It's exactly what I need. Exactly what I deserve on a day like today.

I grab a fork and dive in. I don't even bother to put it on a plate. I'm eating fast, shoving bites of cake in as quickly as possible. I don't want Aunt Laura or Josh to catch me; but more than that, I want the cake to take away this horrible ache in my body. I want that so badly.

The cake plate is empty in a matter of minutes. But I don't stop there.

In the cupboard I find Cheez-Its and shove crackers in by the handful. Above the refrigerator, hidden behind a basket of fresh fruit, I see a Butterfinger (my uncle's one weakness). I grab it and am just turning toward the stairs when I spot the flyer.

It's got a blurry, black-and-white photo of the front of my house, my real house with Dad. Across the top is our address. And below the image are a bunch of details about our house: two bedrooms, one bathroom, a large backyard, walking distance to school. It's described as a "quaint home that needs a little TLC."

With my hands still covered in yellow cheese powder, I pick it up, not caring that I've left orange fingerprints behind.

At the very bottom of the flyer is a price. And then I know. She's going to sell my house.

A partly chewed wad of cheese crackers sits in my mouth, but I can't swallow it. I can't move. Can't breathe.

She's going to sell my house. The house where my mom painted a row of daisies around the top of the kitchen walls. The house with the patched-up window pane in the back from when my dad was teaching me to catch and throw a ball. The house where, if I sneak into my dad's bedroom and push all the way to the back of the closet, I can still kind of smell my mom's perfume among the dust bunnies and moth balls.

I crumple the flyer in my stained hands and throw it far across the room.

Then I grab my backpack, the Butterfinger, and the

Cheez-it box and run up to my room. I'm crying now. But mostly I'm pissed. She can't do this! She can't do this to us!

I slam the door behind me and fling myself onto my bed. For fifteen minutes I down the rest of the food. Then, ready to hurl, I lie back, eyes closed, and try to pretend this isn't happening.

At three forty-five there's a light knock on my door.

"Bennett?" Aunt Laura calls. "You ready to go to your dad's?"

I lie. I tell her I don't feel good (well, that part's true). Head pounding. Need to lie down. Best if you just leave me alone.

I think she doubts my story, but she doesn't press.

Then, for the next hour, I think about my dad. Does he wonder where I am, if something has happened to me? Does he think I'm hurt or sick? He knows I had the meet yesterday. I debate calling him; but honestly, I'm not up to trying to figure out what he's saying over the phone. And I'm definitely not up to being cheerful and encouraging.

I picture him sitting in his chair, looking at the clock. I know the hour he spends with me daily means everything to him.

But I don't want to talk. I don't want to hear about his latest aches and pains, how hard therapy is, what he's accomplished lately.

Because I'm quitting. And how can I explain that to him? Especially when I accused him of that very same thing only a few weeks ago. I can't face the look in his eyes when I tell him.

But I know in my heart I'm done with running. P. G. was right. Luis was right. I'm Fat Boy. And I should stop pretending that I'm not.

CHAPTER 30
When a Dodgers Fan Needs a Giants Fan

Josh knocks lightly on my door a few hours after dinner—a dinner I didn't go down for since all the junk I ate was sitting heavily in my stomach. I've got the John Wooden book open in front of me, but I can't concentrate and keep reading the same sentence over and over. Josh asks if he can get me anything. I pretend to be asleep, and he goes away.

I close the book. Instead of reading, I just lie there trying to imagine my old life. Before cross-country. Before eighth grade. Before my dad's stroke.

It's funny, really. I've been overweight and teased for roughly the last seven years of my life. And in all those years, I rarely felt sorry for myself.

But now my dad's crippled, and the only way to get him uncrippled is to sell the house I've grown up in.

Ignoring my homework and wishing for the easy days of fifth grade, when my biggest issue was not getting picked to play kick ball, I let the tears roll down my cheeks. The light starts to fade outside my window. I feel myself dozing off, still in my running clothes from cross-country.

There's a gentle rapping on my door. Probably Josh again. I close my eyes and ignore it. But it isn't Josh. It's my aunt.

"Bennett?" She gently pushes open the door. I keep my eyes closed and hope she'll get the hint.

She walks over to my bed. "Someone's here to see you."

I open one eye, curious despite myself. Nobody comes to visit me. The kids from Truman live too far away.

"Come on, Bennett," my aunt says, sounding annoyed. "Look, I don't know what happened to you today. But right now, you need to . . ."

". . . get your butt out of bed, bro," says P. G., walking right into my room, flipping on the overhead light. I blink. P. G.'s grinning as if the last few weeks never happened.

"All right then," Aunt Laura says. "I'll leave you two alone."

I sit up, speechless. P. G. grabs my desk chair, tosses my sweats to the floor, and flips one leg over to sit on it backward. He perches his chin on the back of the chair.

"Okay, I'm going to say this quickly and get it over with." He takes a big inhale of air. "You were right. I've been a jerk. A crappy friend. And I'm sorry."

I can't even respond for a second. I blink once. Twice.

"How'd you get here?"

"I had my sister drop me off. She's missed you, man. My whole family has. I've told them you've been busy with your dad. Finally, I leveled with Selena. Man, did she give me an earful! That girl can yell! She agreed to bring me over here tonight if I promised to apologize and not do anything stupid. I've already apologized, and I'm really hoping you'll help me out so I don't have to do anything stupid." He grins.

"But why?" I'm still trying to grasp what he's saying. "You told me just this morning how much I've changed, that you didn't recognize me anymore. Why now?"

"Because it stinks not having you around, okay?" He shrugs his shoulders. "I don't know. When you called me dumb this morning, it stuck with me all day. And I realized you were right. I've been acting real dumb. Here you are with your dad in the hospital, living with your *loco* aunt, trying not to get your butt kicked by that *loco* in the *cabeza* Luis; and I've been giving you a hard time about some stupid cross-country team."

"Yeah, you have." I'm not ready to accept his apology yet, even though I'm really glad to see him. "Cross-country isn't stupid, P. G."

"I know. I know. Listen, I blew it. Can we just, you know, hang out again like old times? It hasn't been easy for me, either! While you've been enjoying lunch with your new running friends, I've been eating alone on a bench near the band room. It sucks, dude."

It hurts to think of him sitting alone every day at lunch. Before finding Mark and Bryce, I did it enough to know how much it really blows. But it doesn't change the fact that P. G. dumped me when I needed him the most.

"I'm glad you came over here," I say. "But I can't just pretend like nothing happened. Pretend you haven't spoken to me in what, like a month?"

"Look, Bennett." P. G. stands up. "I didn't expect you to throw your arms around me in a bear hug; but I didn't expect you to be a jerk, either. The Bennett I know would have accepted the apology, made a joke, and let it go. What's your deal?"

For a moment he glares at me, and I glare back. My anger at the world has a clear target now, and it feels good.

"Dude." His features soften. "You remember that time in third grade when you and me were the only two kids in our class who didn't get invited to Ryan Jackson's birthday party?"

I nod.

"Remember how, without telling you, I went to him at recess and tried to give him my signed Barry Bonds card if he would invite us?"

I chuckle. I can't help it. "Nobody wanted your stupid Barry Bonds card."

"Hey! I'm trying to tell a story here!" He runs a hand through his hair. "Ryan still didn't invite us. And afterward, when you found out what I did, you were so pissed at me. I remember you wouldn't talk to me the whole way home. Finally, when I asked you why you were so mad, you told me that we didn't have to beg people to be our friends. We had each other, and that was all the friends we needed. You remember that?"

I nod again.

"I've thought about that day a lot. Every time somebody gives me a hard time about my weight or when a girl disses me, I think about what you said. You are the only friend I really need. So when you go and join the cross-country team, I start wondering if you've changed your mind. You know? Maybe I'm not good enough for you anymore, see?"

"That's crazy! You'll always be . . ."

He holds up a hand. "Yeah, I get that now. But that's what it felt like. Like you were getting invited to Ryan's party, and I was the one left holding the Barry Bonds card. Alone."

"Man." I shake my head. "That would *really* suck."

P. G. laughs. "You're a butthead. Really and truly a butthead." He sits down on my bed so he faces me.

I laugh.

"Sorry, man. From the minute I woke up this morning, my day has sucked. Big-time. Seeing you in the cafeteria didn't help. Luis is threatening . . . Well, I don't know what he's threatening exactly, but definitely something, because I finally stood up to him today and called him out. My stupid aunt is going to sell my house so we can pay for my dad's rehab. And I pretty much quit cross-country today. Then you walk in here, and I just . . . I don't know . . . lost it, I guess."

"Whoa, dude!" He holds up one palm toward me. "Slow down! You quit cross-country?"

I back up to the beginning and pretty much tell him everything. About my dad's progress, the insurance issues, Luis, and even about Taylor. I finish with the news I got today about there being only five runners for next week's meet and how I feel as if I can't be one of them.

"Benny-man." He leans back and whistles through his teeth. "You got a lot going on."

I laugh. "Yeah."

"So, hold on, bro. Let's think about this. First, Luis." P. G. leans back onto his elbows. "I was talking to Selena about him and how he's such a jerk. Guess what? Turns out his grandma comes into the clinic where Selena works. Apparently, she's his guardian or something. She was complaining big-time about him. She's thinking about sending him to live with his uncle in Phoenix. She said the next time he gets busted, she's going to ship him off."

I consider that news. Makes me feel a little bad for Luis. Kind of. For a second.

"But, Benny-man, you can't quit cross-country. If you bail you'll regret it for the rest of the year, maybe even your life. Look at you, man. You've lost what, like twenty pounds? You're running a couple of miles without stopping? If you quit this team, you'll let them down; but more importantly, you'll let yourself down. Don't be that stupid."

"But don't you get it?" I protest. "If I *do* run, I'll let the team down. I can't get a good score for them. We'll lose, and it'll be my fault."

"And if you don't run, they'll lose, and it'll be your fault. Come on, these guys you're hanging out with? They sound okay. Not as cool as me, but okay. No matter how you do, they're going to be cool with it. But if you bail? Dude, that's unforgivable."

"So, what do I do? Run and come in last?"

"I think this calls for the work of Coach P. G." He raises his eyebrows and wiggles them up and down.

"Uh, yeah, right." I raise my own eyebrows at him. "Coach P. G., who can't run down the stairs? That Coach P. G.?"

"Yep, the one and the same." He lifts his chin. "Dude, I can't run, but I can time you. I can yell at your butt to move faster. I can throw you a bottle of water and then get you running again. We got what? A week? Let's train your butt off."

I laugh. He has no clue what he's talking about. But at least he's talking to me again. If he wants to coach me, why not? It can't hurt. I'm going to lose, anyway.

And he's right about one thing: I can't quit. Maybe he won't be such a bad coach after all.

CHAPTER 31
Forgiveness

P. G. leaves, promising to be at my aunt's house at six thirty the next morning.

I feel ten pounds lighter, like actual weights have been removed from my shoulders. The thought of next week's race still makes me want to puke, but at least I'll be puking with P. G. by my side.

I hustle downstairs to grab a turkey sandwich. Now that all the sugar and trans fat and stuff has settled in my stomach, I'm craving something healthy.

My aunt's at the kitchen sink, washing dinner dishes.

She turns around when I walk in. "You and P. G. okay?"

My body stiffens, seeing her. I wonder if she's found the crumpled-up flyer of my house. The empty cake pan.

"Is that what was bugging you all afternoon?" she asks.

For a second I won't look at her. I contemplate ignoring her altogether and stomping back up to my room. But then a whoosh of exhaustion floods my body. I'm tired of avoiding everything. Tired of running away.

"Did you really hate my dad for killing my mom?"

I don't know where the question came from. It wasn't what I was planning to ask. But just as quickly, I realize it's the question I've always wanted to ask her.

Aunt Laura freezes. Then she slowly dries her hands on a towel and comes over to sit at the kitchen table. She motions for me to sit next to her. I don't move. She takes a deep breath.

"Well, okay. This wasn't where I thought this conversation would go, but . . ." She looks down at her lap and then back up at me.

"When I found out your mom had cancer, Bennett, I was devastated. I knew she'd been sick. But I was preoccupied with being a mom to Kiley and Josh, who were still pretty little. I didn't take time to figure out why Leah was tired so much. Plus, she made excuses not to see me, so it wasn't like I was really 'seeing' what was going on. When I did see her, she'd put on a happy face and pretend she was fine."

Though I don't remember much from that time, I can picture my mom smiling through the pain.

"Then a few months before she died, she finally told me what was going on. I was so angry. Angry at her for not telling me. Angry at myself for not seeing it. Angry at your dad for not being honest with me. It seemed like she just gave up. There were treatment options, but she said she didn't want them—they made her feel sick and even more tired, and they weren't working, anyway. I pleaded with her to keep trying, but she was resolved. That was the thing about your mom; when she made up her mind, that was it."

"Yeah." I shift my weight. Look at my feet.

"But your dad. As long as I've known him, Paul has always been Mr. Calm, Cool, and Collected. He doesn't get angry. And he seemed to accept all this stuff with Leah so easily. Almost like he didn't care."

I feel anger bubble up. "That's not—!"

She holds up her hand. "I know, Bennett. Looking back, I know that wasn't true. But at the time I just hated that he wasn't pushing her. And I really needed someone to hate, Bennett. I needed someone to blame. Paul pulled me aside one day and told me that my badgering Leah wasn't helping her. He suggested I let it go and spend as much time with her as I could. He told me about some holistic remedies—like herbs and acupuncture and yoga—that she was doing, which were helping a little. But I lost it. How could that stuff keep my sister alive?"

"That's why you screamed at him that day. The day of the funeral." I look right at her.

"Yes, Bennett. The day of her funeral, I was angry and so hurt. I kept thinking that if I had known about her cancer earlier, I could have saved her. That was stupid, Bennett. I want you to know that. Nothing could have saved your mom. Not chemo, not drugs, not surgery. By the time she found it, it was already too late. But when you're grieving, you think stupid things."

She's quiet for a second.

"One of the stupidest thoughts I had was that your dad was responsible. I accused him of not being a man and taking care of his wife. I accused him of keeping secrets from me and everybody else so he could keep her to himself. And I accused him of killing your mom."

Tears are running down her face, but she doesn't wipe them away.

I believe what she's saying. But it doesn't make it any easier to forgive her.

"You said some pretty rotten things to my dad," I say softly.

"I'm not proud of it, Bennett." She won't look away from me. Her nose is getting all red and puffy.

I think of my dad standing between me and my aunt, shielding me from her hate and anger. I think of him hugging me reassuringly, telling me it would all be all right. I picture him slumped in his chair the day of his stroke, so helpless.

I also think back to earlier this afternoon. Deciding not to go see him because I was too wrapped up in me. I see my dad sitting alone in his chair, watching the door and waiting for me. How could I have been so selfish? My chest aches. I was such a jerk.

We do stupid things when we're upset and feeling hopeless.

"I was wrong, Bennett." Aunt Laura swipes at a few tears on her cheek. "So wrong. About a week ago I went to see your dad and apologized for the way I'd acted during that time. And your dad, being the kind of guy he is, forgave me—told me he'd actually forgiven me years earlier. One of the best things about your dad is his ability to let stuff go."

I smile. "Yeah."

"Your dad and I will never be best friends. Too much has gone on between us for that. But I'm comfortable with his forgiveness, and I've forgiven myself. We both miss your mom terribly, so much that it physically hurts sometimes. It's one of the reasons that having you here for these past few weeks has been . . ." She pauses and sucks in a shaky breath. "It's been really neat, Bennett. Getting to know you and seeing so much of Leah in you. You are one incredible kid."

I don't feel incredible. I feel overwhelmed and really, really tired.

"I don't want to sell my house," I say.

She pushes her hair from her eyes. "I know."

"Then why are you doing it? Why did you have a flyer made up? You didn't even ask me!" I'm yelling now. Angry. It feels good. "Uncle Jim told me all about the insurance. *He* trusts me, at least! But you can't sell my house! It's the one thing that . . ." I gulp and try to find the words. "It's the one place that still reminds me of Mom." I drop my voice and my chin. "You can't sell it, okay?"

For a second the room is dead silent. I hear the ticking of the big grandfather clock in the entryway.

"We're not selling your house, Bennett."

I dare to look up at her.

"Your dad put his foot down on that, too." She gives a small smile.

"My dad knows what's going on?"

"He didn't at first. But your uncle Jim and I decided we needed to talk to him about the different options. He found out last week."

"Why didn't anyone tell me? Why wasn't I in on this conversation? It's my life, too."

Aunt Laura shrugs. "You're probably right. We should have asked you to be a part of that conversation. I guess we were all trying to protect you." Her eyes take on a pained look. "Seems like we didn't do a very good job."

I don't say anything for a minute.

"You know, Aunt Laura," I say slowly, "you've done a lot for me in this past month and a half. Letting me stay here and driving me to school every day and all that. But you don't ever really ask me about stuff before you make a decision. Like going to my old school instead of Meadowbrook. Or running with Uncle Jim in the mornings. It isn't that either of those things is horrible. It's that you didn't ask me what I think."

She pauses. Her eyes narrow. She purses her lips. Here it comes. The Aunt Laura I've grown to know and . . . hate.

But she surprises me.

"I guess I understand that. I was just trying to do what was best for you."

"But sometimes what's best for me is letting *me* decide what's best for me. Does that make sense?"

Her nod is slow and deliberate.

"Yes, it does."

We just look at each other for a long, stretched-out minute, both of us red eyed and sniffling.

"So, how are we going to pay for my dad's rehab?"

"Your dad wants to get a loan. You can use your house as collateral, and you should be able to get enough money to cover it. The rehab place is giving Paul an extension to give him time to get the loan processed. He knows he's going to have to work hard to get out of there by Christmas, when the insurance expires completely. But he's pretty determined." She smiles. "Like someone else I know."

I want to smile, but I have to look away. She doesn't know how close I was to quitting today. I'm so grateful to P. G. for showing up when he did.

She stands and stretches. "You good with all this, Bennett?"

"Yeah, I think so." I start to move toward the refrigerator and then stop. "Hey, Aunt Laura?"

She turns at the doorway to look at me.

"If my dad has forgiven you, then, uh, I just want you to know that, well, it's all cool with me, too."

She blinks. Bites her bottom lip.

"Thank you," she says softly, and heads up the stairs to her room.

• • •

An hour later, my homework is tucked neatly in my folder and I'm once again lying in bed.

Then it hits me that there's still one last thing I need to do.

I pad quietly down the hallway to Josh's room and rap my knuckles lightly on his door.

"Yeah?" I hear him call.

I poke my head in his room. He's in bed, reading. He smiles when he sees me.

"Hey, Bennett. You feeling better?"

I nod. "But listen, Josh. I was a jerk to you this morning in the car. I'll listen to your speech tomorrow, okay?"

Josh grins, and I swear it touches both ears. "That'd be great, Bennett."

"We're good?"

He nods. "We're always good, Bennett. But yeah, we're good."

I close his door and smile my way back to my room.

CHAPTER 32
Operation: Get Bennett Faster

Promptly at six thirty the next morning, P. G. shows up at Aunt Laura's wearing big, baggy basketball shorts, a gigantic T-shirt, and a whistle. He still looks half asleep.

P. G. consults his clipboard and decides I should do some speed work for half an hour. He stands at one end of my street with a stopwatch. On his go, I run really hard down the whole block. When I arrive at his end of the block, panting and close to death, he gives me my time: three minutes and twenty-nine seconds.

"Good job, man."

Then he insists I shave a second or two off of it the next time.

By the fifth time I'm sure my legs are going to fall off and I've busted a lung. P. G. calls it a day and leads me inside, where he gobbles up my aunt's blueberry-and-buckwheat waffles—"These aren't half bad, man!"— while I take a shower. My aunt drops us off, saying, "Hope to see you tomorrow, P. G."

I'm not sure this is a good thing.

At lunch I bring P. G. to meet Mark and Bryce. P. G. is pretty quiet even though Mark and Bryce immediately accept him as if he's been there all along. Hopefully, he'll relax with them over time.

Mark asks if we both want to come to his house to swim on Sunday afternoon. In the past I've stayed away from pool parties. Me and swim trunks don't work out so well. But I find myself saying, "Sure, we'll be there."

For the first time in my life I feel like I belong to a group. I have P. G. back, *and* I have this cool new group of guys to hang out with. Man, I feel lucky.

When the bell rings, P. G. and I start toward fifth period laughing like old times.

"Ah, the Fat Boys are reunited!" Luis calls from down the hallway. But quick as lightning, he's right up in my face.

"Don't matter who you got hanging around you, Fat Boy," he spits at me. "I'll still take you out."

"Whatever, Luis. You don't scare me."

P. G. stands right next to me. "I got his back, dude. Know that." P. G.'s chin is up defiantly.

For a second no one moves. I size up my large, determined best friend next to scrawny little Luis, who is for once solo. It's no contest. And Luis must figure this out, too, because he says, "Whatever. Your mistake, Fat Boys." He snaps his gum in my face, spits it out on my shoe, and walks away.

I kick the gum off. To P. G. I say, "Gum on my shoe? That's his idea of a threat?"

P. G. laughs. "Well said, Fat Boy."

I smile. "I'm learning, Fat Boy Junior."

"Who you calling Junior?" P. G. asks. "You're the one down a few pounds!"

"Good point. Maybe you should be Fat Boy Senior. I'll let Luis know next time we see him."

P. G. grins and flexes his arm, which really doesn't flex a whole lot.

• • •

Cross-country practice is hard that day. My legs are sore from the morning. And because I didn't get much sleep last night, I'm pooped. We do a two-and-a-half-mile run through some streets around the school. I hang with some of the slower sixth-grade runners in the back of the pack and finish with them in about twenty-five minutes. That's actually my fastest time and my longest run so far. But it takes everything I have.

Uncle Jim drops me off at my dad's at four o'clock on the nose. As soon as I walk into my dad's room, Jameel greets me. I can tell by the look on his face that something's up.

"Your dad was about to jump out of his skin waiting for you to show up." Jameel grins and walks over to my dad, who's sitting in his wheelchair.

"Ready, Paul?"

"Ready," my dad says clearly and firmly. But his upper

lip is beaded with sweat. He's nervous.

Jameel hooks his arms underneath my dad's armpits. Slowly, he lifts my dad from his chair. Dad rises unsteadily, gripping the arms of his chair until the last second.

"You tell me when," Jameel says as my dad stands fully upright.

For a few long seconds my dad teeters there, leaning on Jameel's strong arms for support.

"Now."

Jameel lets my dad go and reaches for a walker that's tucked in the corner of the room. He sets it in front of my dad, who gratefully leans forward and grips its handles.

With painful slowness, my dad's left foot scoots forward. He loses his balance for a second, and it looks as if his arms might buckle; but then Jameel is right there to steady him.

"Dad! That's—" I start, but Jameel stops me with a hand.

Without looking up at me, my dad once again grips the walker and pushes his right leg forward. He's now standing with both feet together, having taken one full step. My dad is walking!

The room is silent. I can hear the whoosh of the air conditioner and the grinding of ancient water pipes somewhere in the building. But my eyes never leave my dad.

His face screws up in concentration. He inches his left foot forward again, followed by his right foot. He looks up at me like a child who just hit his first home run. But then he loses his balance and begins to pitch forward. Jameel is quick as lightning, hauling my dad upright.

"Bennett, push that chair toward us, will you?"

I hurry and do it.

My dad is seated again, breathing heavily but obviously proud.

"Dad! That was unbelievable!" I say, slapping his back.

Jameel grabs my dad's right hand and leads him through some complicated handshake that ends in them bopping knuckles.

I roll my eyes and put my hands on my hips like I've seen Kiley do. "Those handshakes are so yesterday!" I say with exaggerated disgust.

Everyone cracks up. Jameel heads out after that, leaving the two of us alone.

"Dad?"

He looks up at me.

"I know about the insurance thing."

My dad's eyes widen. "Bennett," he says carefully. "I was going to tell you . . ."

". . . once you had it all worked out," I finish. "I know. But we could have worked it out quicker if we'd been working together."

He looks at me hard. "Did Laura . . . tell you we're going to take out a second loan . . . on the house?" His breaths are still labored after those few steps he took.

I nod.

"It's going to make things tight for a while." He pauses and wipes some sweat from his upper lip. "Paying this off. Me not getting a full paycheck for a few months." Another pause. Another deep breath. "And college is not that far away for you. . . ."

I laugh and hold up my hand. "Jeez! Dad! Let's worry about one thing at a time, okay?"

He smiles sheepishly.

"We'll make it," I say softly, looking down at my hands. "Yeah, we will."

I know what I want to do. Something I never did before my dad's stroke. Quickly, before I can change my mind, I lean forward and hug him. His scratchy, unshaven cheek rubs against mine; and I smell his familiar musky, sweaty smell. I grab around his shoulders and squeeze. And to my surprise, he brings both of his arms up and squeezes back.

• • •

The next morning is Saturday, and Uncle Jim drops me off at P. G.'s so we can continue our training. Mrs. Gomez fusses over me so much that I'm actually embarrassed.

"Ah, come here, *mijo*! Let me look at you. You're so skinny! Are they not feeding you?" She holds me by the shoulders. She's just about my height, so we see eye to eye. "Come. I've got some warm, fresh tortillas. I've made some cookies, too."

I break my "healthy eating" for the afternoon and gobble up everything Mrs. Gomez sets in front of me.

Selena gets home while I'm polishing off one last cookie, kisses me on the cheek, and asks how my running is going. P. G.'s *abuela* wanders in and insists I give her a hug.

"My handsome Ben-ito," she says in her thickly accented English as she pats my cheek.

I've missed this family so much.

We chill for a while after my pig-out session to let everything settle. Then P. G. grabs his stopwatch and his bike while I get changed. Today I'm going to run three miles. I'm going to start very slowly and increase my effort every half mile. The last mile I will run all out. P. G.'s house is on flatter ground than my aunt's, so I won't have to deal with any hills. But it's going to be tough.

Mrs. Gomez kisses my cheek and promises to have cold water ready when I get back.

"Not cold, Mama," P. G. says. "Cold isn't good for your body after you run."

I look at him surprised. "How do you know that?"

He looks a little defensive. "I got the Internet, too. I'm your coach now, man. It's my job to know this stuff."

Before we leave Mrs. Gomez hugs me. "I'm proud of you, Bennett. You do good today."

It's a long three miles; but it helps having P. G. on his bike right beside me, calling out my time and handing me a water bottle when we stop to let cars pass. By the last mile I'm giving it everything I have, running a nine-minute-mile pace, faster than I've ever run. I know P. G.

being there has a lot to do with it.

I pace his driveway to cool down while he shouts out my stats. "Ten-minute-mile average. Your fastest pace was about seven thirty, when you were sprinting across that driveway because that dog came after you. Still, you did a good job, man."

The next morning P. G. shows up at my aunt's house ready to train me. He has his bike with him and rides along next to me again, silently keeping track of my times and calling out encouragement every so often. I run nearly three miles at an average pace of 9:45 minutes per mile. I'm getting faster.

And I'm getting nervous.

"Listen, B.," P. G. says after the run on Sunday morning. "You're getting this. A couple more days of training, and you're going to be fine."

He's taken his job seriously. P. G. seems to know more about running and training than I do. Will I ever get him out here running with me? I hope so. We could run cross-country in high school together.

P. G. stays at my aunt's until it's time to go to Mark's house to swim. A lot of the cross-country kids are there, including Kendra. At first P. G. and I can't get up the courage to take off our shirts and jump in. But after a few minutes P. G. just flings off his T-shirt and cannonballs into the pool. Shrugging, I follow him a minute later, minus the cannonball.

I can tell P. G. is instantly in love. His eyes follow

Kendra everywhere she goes. Within minutes he's got the crowd in the palm of his hand, cracking jokes and showing off in the pool.

When the pizza arrives, P. G. and I grab our towels and some pizza, and sit under the palm trees. Mark and Bryce plop down with us a few minutes later.

"So, Bennett, there's this killer rumor at school that you got a thing for Taylor Hunter," says Bryce, his mouth full of pizza.

I feel my face grow warm. Suddenly, the pizza in my mouth seems hard to swallow.

"You've seen her, dude," I say. "She ain't gonna like a guy like me."

"Why not?" Mark asks, no trace of humor in his voice.

"Because I'm . . . well . . ."

". . . a dope when it comes to chicks," P. G. finishes for me. I shoot him a look of gratitude. "Bennett starts talking about things like algebra formulas and baseball whenever a girl gets close. You gotta help him, dude." P. G. shakes his head in mock disappointment.

Our small group laughs comfortably.

Kendra slides her towel next to Mark and flops down. "What's so funny?" she asks, setting her plate carefully on her folded legs.

"Bennett's got a thing for Taylor Hunter," says Bryce.

"Bryce! That's not—" I start to say.

"Good taste, Bennett." Kendra nods. "She's cute *and* smart."

I can't believe they're talking as if me getting together with Taylor is anything but wishful thinking. Can they not see this spare tire I have for a stomach?

I'm relieved when Bryce changes the subject.

"So, P. G.," he says casually, "when you gonna start running with us?"

"When Bennett stops rooting for the stupid Dodgers and becomes a Giants fan." He doesn't look up.

"Seriously, dude." Bryce takes a bite of pizza. "It's a lot of fun."

P. G. shifts uncomfortably.

"P. G. has allergies," I say with exaggerated seriousness.

"Really?" Kendra looks at me suspiciously.

"Yeah, he's allergic to sweat."

She sighs and shakes her head in disgust.

P. G. looks thoughtful, and he spends the rest of lunch trying to charm Kendra.

I'm thinking that P. G. on the cross-country team is a definite possibility.

CHAPTER 33
Plate Time

All too soon it's Thursday morning, the day of the meet. My stomach's doing this really uncomfortable somersault thing. I try to sleep in, but my body is so used to getting up at six thirty that I wake up early, anyway. I run through some stretches, hoping it will calm me down.

Aunt Molly texts me good luck and tells me that she's planning to come see me run at the finals, which, if we do well today, are in about a week. *If we do well today.* Translation: if *I* do well today. I swallow the lump of fear rising in my throat.

Aunt Laura has a big, nourishing breakfast for me: scrambled eggs, low-fat ham, and whole wheat toast. Uncle Jim jogs down the stairs, grabs a piece of toast, and casually hands me a small, flat, wrapped package.

"What's this?" I put down my fork. Aunt Laura wipes her hands on her apron and turns to look at me expectantly. Kiley tells whoever is on the other end of her cell phone call to hang on a second. How is it possible that she's on the phone this early in the morning?

"Open it!" Josh urges.

Totally taken by surprise, I pull apart the taped ends.

Inside is a small framed picture of Josh and me at my first cross-country meet. I look sweaty and tired. But there's this satisfaction in my eyes. Josh has his hand on my shoulder and is staring at me with admiration and something else, something that makes my chest tighten a little. On the frame are the engraved words:

Do not let what you cannot do interfere with what you can do. —John Wooden

I look up at my uncle, speechless.

"He was a coach at—" Uncle Jim starts to explain.

"UCLA." I gape at him. "Basketball. I know. I've been reading his book."

"Really?" Uncle Jim looks impressed. "Then you know he's one of the most respected basketball coaches ever. Maybe in any sport."

"Yeah, I know." I finger the letters of the quote. "This means a lot, you guys. I . . . just . . . well, thank you."

"We'll be there this afternoon to cheer you on, sport," Uncle Jim says. "You're a good runner. You got this." He squeezes my shoulder on the way out the door.

I look at the picture one more time. A runner. A *good* runner.

• • •

Throughout the day I force myself to drink as much water as I can. This means I have to stop in the bathroom between every class. I see other cross-country runners in there, too. We're all "peeing clear."

Taylor has made me a bag of these cookies she says are supposed to be full of energy and great to eat before a run. "My dad is a cyclist, and he eats these things by the dozen when he's training. I guess they're what Lance Armstrong ate when he was racing in the Tour de France."

I take the bag from her. "Thanks."

"So, I'll see you at the race, okay?"

My eyes widen and my heart stops beating. "You're really coming?"

She grins. "I told you I was! You need cheerleaders, right?"

I have a cheerleader. A cute one. Wow.

By lunch I'm actually feeling good. Jittery, but confident, too. The weather is perfect: about seventy degrees with a light wind. I'm hydrated and relaxed and *ready*.

I've forgotten all about Luis. Unfortunately, he hasn't forgotten about me.

CHAPTER 34
When a Guy's Gotta Pee . . .

Halfway through fifth period I have to pee so badly, I know I'm not going to make it until class is over. Fortunately, we have a sub who could care less about the classroom rule of no bathroom breaks.

I grab the hall pass on my way out the door and make a beeline for the closest restroom. I'm rounding the corner of the hallway, nearly jogging since my bladder's about to burst, when I bump right into another kid, knocking him clean off his feet.

"Hey!" He falls back into some lockers.

"Sorry, man . . ." I stop when I realize who I'm reaching out my hand to.

He realizes it, too. He ignores my hand and pushes himself up on his own.

"Watch where you're going, Fat Boy!" Luis's lips curl up into a sneer.

His voice makes my stomach clench. I start to walk

on. I am not in the mood for his crap. I also don't want to pee my pants.

But, of course, Luis jumps at this rare opportunity. Like a snake, he slithers up next to me. "So where we going, Fat Boy? Sneaking out for an afternoon snack? Mom didn't pack you enough lunch?"

I'm doing a pretty good job of ignoring him. I'm about two steps from the bathroom door when it dawns on him where I'm headed. He immediately jumps between me and the door, blocking my path.

"Aha!" He raises his eyebrows. "Fat Boy has to pee. How bad? How long can you hold it?" He continues to stand in my path and pretends to check his watch as if he has all the time in the world.

I don't have all the time in the world. My bladder feels like a beach ball.

I try to shove past him. I'm bigger than he is, but he sees it coming and grabs onto each side of the doorway and braces himself.

"Touch me again and you're dead, Fat Boy."

"Stay where you are, and you're going to smell like pee for the rest of the day, Luis."

For a second he looks uncertain. Then his sneer returns. "You wouldn't. You don't have the guts to do it right here. Go ahead; I dare you."

Too late I realize I can't back down. So I start to unbutton my pants like I mean business. I'm seriously praying that a) no one comes by and sees me getting ready to strip, and b) Luis will move before this goes too far.

He cackles and stands his ground.

I doggedly unzip my jeans. I reach for the button and notice that Luis is grabbing for something in his pocket. My heart is hammering. If he pulls out a knife, what the heck am I going to do? Really pee on him? Run? Scream?

At that moment I hear voices. Deep ones. Grown-up ones.

I zip up quickly and turn around, right as the principal, assistant principal, and a campus aid come striding around the corner.

My heart is beating as if it wants to escape my chest. Here I am, out of class, looking guilty, and standing next to Luis of all people. Did they see me zipping up my pants?

Luis relaxes his stance and drops his arms, trying to look as if we've only been chatting outside the boys' bathroom.

"What are you both doing out of class?" Mr. Burton, the principal, demands.

I hold up the hall pass from Mr. Morrison's. "Uh, just trying to use the bathroom."

Luis shrugs, probably hoping they'll assume he's with me. Shyeah, right. Me and Luis—buds from way back.

"Who's in there?" asks Mr. Burton, gesturing toward the bathroom.

"I don't know," I answer quickly. "I haven't gone in yet."

The campus aid points at Luis. "I'm sure he's one of them. He's been busted for doing this before."

One of them? One of *who*? Busted for doing what?

"What? Me? I didn't do nothing!" Luis is using a high-pitched voice I've never heard before. "I was going to use the bathroom!"

"How long have you been here, son?" Mr. Burton asks me.

"Um, just got here, really."

"Did you see anyone come out of this bathroom?"

Suddenly, the door to the bathroom flies open, smacking the wall; and three boys stumble out, laughing. They stop short when they see the five of us. Quickly, they sober up and try to keep walking past us as if nothing is unusual.

"Hey, Luis," one says casually. Luis glares back at him.

The campus aid moves in front of them. "Where are you three headed so fast?"

"Back to class," says the shortest one.

"Really? Whose class?" she asks.

He pauses for the briefest of seconds. "Morrison's."

Bad move. I'm standing there holding a big wooden block that says HALL PASS MR. MORRISON on it. There's only one hall pass in each classroom, and I've got it.

"Bennett, is this kid in your class right now?" asks Mr. Burton.

I don't like ratting out other kids, but he leaves me no choice. "Uh, no, I don't think so."

The assistant principal has gone into the bathroom and emerges with a grim expression. She's blinking her eyes, which are red and irritated. And coming from the bathroom is the most god-awful smell of rotten eggs mixed in with something really sweet. Even Luis makes a face.

"Stink bombs, graffiti, and what looks like it could be pot," she remarks.

"Come on, boys," says Mr. Burton to the three kids. "Guess we've got some phone calls to make."

He turns to Luis. "You, too, Luis."

Luis gets wide-eyed. "Wait! I didn't have anything to do with this! I came to use the bathroom. I swear!"

Now, here's the thing. I don't know where Luis came from when I met him in the hallway a few minutes ago. It could have been from this bathroom. But I'll say this: those three boys reek of whatever mess they've been making in that bathroom. Luis, on the other hand, smells like he always does: cheap cologne and moth balls. Maybe a little cigarette smoke.

If I stay quiet, it's probably his third strike. He might get sent away if his grandma makes good on her threat. That gets him out of my hair permanently.

But it's wrong.

"He wasn't in there with them," I say to Mr. Burton.

"He was out here with me the whole time. We walked over together."

Luis turns to look at me, his eyes narrow, distrustful. I'm sure he can't figure out why I would save him.

"All right, then," says Mr. Burton. "Find another bathroom to use. This one's off limits for the day."

I start down the hallway. I'm close to exploding at this point. Every step hurts.

I hear Luis fall in step next to me.

I stop and glare down at him. "Look," I say, irritated. "If you're going to stand between me and another bathroom, you are definitely going to get sprayed. I've got about two gallons of water in me, and I'm in misery. I don't want to do it, but I will."

There's silence for a moment. Our eyes are locked.

His hand slides into his pocket.

I tense.

Then he takes the smallest step backward. And drops his eyes from mine.

Quickly, I turn and stride into the bathroom. In a few seconds it's the sweetest relief I've felt all day. Maybe all month.

CHAPTER 35
The Rock

I'm staring out at the course at Meadowbrook.

"Coach said it wasn't flat. He didn't say we'd be running uphill!" I whine to Mark and Bryce as we drop our stuff by the finish line. I should've guessed that it would be hilly.

They laugh. "It's Meadowbrook, dude!" Bryce says, slapping my shoulder. "Nobody told you what they call the last hill on this course?"

"Uh, no." I narrow my eyes. "You want to tell me?"

Bryce and Mark look at each other and grin. "Poop Out!" they yell in unison.

Crap.

There are four schools at this meet: us, Meadowbrook, and two schools I've never heard of. The real competitor is Meadowbrook, who look fierce in their black-and-yellow running jerseys. They have some of the top runners in the valley, according to Coach. Beating them today will secure us a place in the finals.

The races start on time. Our sixth graders perform well. The girls place second and possibly first, since there are rumors that one of the runners for Meadowbrook cut a cone and may be disqualified. The sixth-grade boys grab a first-place finish, no problem. They're running like a well-oiled machine.

I'm feeling like a rubber band that's been stretched to its limits. About to snap.

P. G. trots over as soon as the Gomez family arrives, right before the seventh-and-eighth-grades girls' race.

"How you feel, Benny-man? You hydrated? Warmed up? Stretched?" He has a clipboard, and a pencil between his teeth. "You remember our plan, right? Nine-minute pace on the downs, ten on the ups."

I laugh, even though my stomach is in knots. Who would've ever guessed that P. G. and I would be having this conversation today?

"I got it, Coach."

Mr. Gomez couldn't make it since he's still at work, but Mrs. Gomez and Selena are here. Both kiss my cheek and wish me good luck.

As the girls' race starts, Coach Mendoza calls over the five of us who are in the last race. He explains that the score from the Meadowbrook girl is going to stand.

We moan, but he hushes us.

"Hey, we worry about things we can control. Right now we can control how we run in these last races. The sixth-grade boys got us a solid first. If our girls in this next race can get some decent numbers, we might pull this off."

As the girls round the bend for their first lap, we call out encouragement. Kendra leads our pack of girls. There are a few runners ahead of them, though. They have to pick it up if we're going to take first or even second.

"Looking good, Kendra!" I shout.

"Oh, yeah!" P. G. is right behind me. "Looking very good, girl!"

This is going to be close. Every school has at least one runner in the top five.

After all our girls pass, we grab our numbers from Coach.

"Listen, guys," he says quietly. "Run like we've trained. Help each other out. If you see something your teammate might not, like a guy who's coming up to pass, tell him. Short strides on the uphill and let loose on the downs. Mostly, breathe and stay focused. And, oh yeah, enjoy the run, okay?"

I head toward the start line. And for a second the noise and cheers fade away. I see only my dad.

He's in a wheelchair being pushed by Uncle Jim, jostling over uneven ground. His eyes are glued to me, and he has the biggest smile on his face, though it still sags on the left a little. Trailing behind him are my aunt, Josh, and even Kiley (who is busy texting—what a shocker).

I think back to that moment not long ago when I thought I would have been embarrassed to have my dad here. When I worried what other kids would think of my incapacitated father. My obese dad.

But all that fills me at this moment is gratitude. And a warm lightness that tickles my nervous stomach and pushes my lips into a wide grin.

When I get close, my dad smiles and holds out a tightly closed fist.

"You're here," I say. I tap his knuckles with mine. His hand is almost steady.

"We wanted to surprise you," my dad says. "You ready?"

"I think so."

"You're ready," he says.

Coach Mendoza walks up. "Hey, Bennett, you gotta get to the start line. This your family?"

"Yep." I watch his eyes travel over my dad. His doesn't even blink.

"Nice to meet you all. But now one of our key runners needs to line up."

We divide into our two lines at the start: Bryce and Mark in front, Kaleem and Eduardo each second. I take my spot behind Eduardo. Mark tells us to do a few striders—where we sprint out for maybe twenty yards or so and then jog back to the start line.

Mark leans toward us. "Just keep running. That's all you got to do." Easy for him to say.

Coach comes jogging over. "The girls did well. You guys pull off a second place overall, and we're in the finals, baby!"

We all put our fists into a tight little huddle, and on Mark's count yell, "Truman!"

It's time. I look down at my legs and will them not to fail me. I look up and see P. G. He mouths, "Plate time."

Then, as the course marshal reviews the last-minute instructions, this wimpy-looking runner from Meadowbrook leans over and says, "Hey, Fatso, you really gonna run today? Somebody promise you a hot fudge sundae at the finish line?"

The color drains from my face. *Fatso*. After all I've done to get this far, I'm still Fat Boy.

My confidence is sucked out of me. I know then that no matter how much training I've done, I can't compete with these guys. I look down at my shoes—now worn and dirty from all the miles I've put on them.

"He's gonna kick your puny butt. Just watch him." It's Mark's voice.

My head snaps up. Mark and Bryce are glaring at this kid as if he's Public Enemy Number 1.

But the Meadowbrook kid laughs and flings his shaggy hair away from his face. "We'll see, I guess, huh? Unless it's too dark when he finishes!"

He cackles and slaps a high five with the kid next to him.

That's when a rush of adrenaline hits me. I look at this short little kid who needs a haircut, and I want more than anything to beat him. I've never felt this before. This intense competitiveness.

"You afraid I might beat you?" The words are out before I've even thought them through. The kid looks up at me surprised. Mark and Bryce smirk.

"You better watch it, buddy," Bryce says. "My boy B.'s not afraid of anything."

I feel energy coursing through my legs. Maybe those cookies from Taylor are loaded with steroids or something. I'm strong and ready. So ready.

On the gun blast I let my legs go, and we're off. I settle in. I see P. G. check his watch and give me the thumbs-up.

The first half mile is a piece of cake. I'm pretty sure I'm running faster than a ten-minute pace. It's downhill, so I let momentum and gravity do some of the work for me. I'm ahead of about a dozen other runners; but I know that once we start climbing, I'll really have to work.

My legs feel it the instant we move from downhill to uphill. I shorten my stride a little, just like Coach said, and try to keep my pace steady. My breathing kicks up a notch. It's hard to keep an "in-two-three, out-two three" rhythm. But I'm determined to stay focused.

I'm almost to the mile marker. I can hear the crowds cheering. I try hard to breathe evenly and smooth out my strides.

For a few moments I feel strong. My legs do what

they're supposed to, and my chest rises and falls.

I see P. G. looking back and forth from me to his watch, nodding his head and pumping his fist. He yells, "You got this, Bennett! You got it! Nine minutes and thirty-six seconds."

I just keep running.

When I pass my dad, I have to look at him. He claps and shouts. Aunt Laura and Uncle Jim stand behind his wheelchair, doing the same. Taylor is a little ways off cheering and yelling. Josh is going nuts. Even Kiley seems to have unglued herself from her phone long enough to holler, "Go, Bennett!"

They are all here for me. Adrenaline kicks in again.

So does gravity. I'm cruising downhill. I'm more than halfway through this race. No side cramps. Things are looking good. I loosen up my stride and let go.

I don't see the rock.

CHAPTER 36
Finishing What I Started

As far as rocks go, it's fairly big. But it's hidden among hunks of grass. I'm looking straight ahead, wondering if I can pass the runner in front of me, when my left foot hits it. My ankle turns inward. A sharp pain shoots up my leg.

I don't fall, but I stumble.

When I place the weight on my left foot, it's excruciating, like someone is taking a knife and twisting it into my ankle. Every step is another twist. I keep moving forward, trying to put more weight on my right foot.

It's bad. I don't know if my ankle is sprained or just twisted. All I know is, it hurts. Tears spring to my eyes. I don't want it to end like this. After a month of running, training with P. G. My whole family here watching. I don't want to limp across that finish line, last place, a loser again.

Less than a half mile to go. I'm going uphill, but it's not too steep.

My team is counting on me. I have to keep running. From somewhere deep, deep within me, I find a reserve of strength I didn't know I had. *I can do this.*

I don't know what will become of my ankle, but I'm going to do this. I have to.

Pain jolts through me with each step. I keep running. The runner I'd hoped to catch up to has widened the distance between us. I'm not sure I can catch him. But I have at least a dozen runners behind me, and I'm not going to let any of them pass.

My eyes are wet but not from tears. Sweat pours down my forehead. The pain is intense. I mutter, "Run, just run." Over and over, "Run, just run."

With a quarter mile to go, the pain eases up a little. Not much, but enough to make me hopeful that my ankle's twisted and not sprained. Or maybe my body is going numb.

I focus straight ahead. The ankle has to wait. I'm finishing this race.

I hold my pace and concentrate on that same runner ahead of me. I'm only about ten paces behind him now, so I'm catching up.

He's from Meadowbrook; I can tell by his jersey.

And then it hits me. It's the guy who called me Fatso before the race. The small kid with the long, shaggy hair. Only ten paces ahead.

I dig in. Amazingly, the ankle holds, though it hurts like crazy. I have some gas left. As the finish line comes into view, I start to use it up. Inch by inch, I gain on him. I'm pumping my arms like mad. I suck in air, just like I used to when I first started running. Only now it's because I'm sprinting.

I want this.

I am a runner. I am not Fat Boy.

My whole body hurts. I'm giving it everything. My arms pump, my stride rate is high. My breathing sounds as if I'm hyperventilating.

I refuse to give up.

P. G. is running alongside the course. I'm that close to the end. "GO! GO! GO, BENNETT! GO!"

I'm also closing in on my opponent. I can almost touch the back of his jersey.

The finish line is maybe ten yards ahead when he turns his head and realizes I'm there. His eyes widen. He sees exactly who I am. He knows.

It's all I need.

In turning to look at me, he lost maybe half a second. I push my legs like never before, stretch my body forward, and with one great, leaping stride, cross that line a half second before him. I hear his grunt as we both slow down.

I gasp for breath. Waves of pain shoot through me. My legs wobble.

And then the world goes black.

CHAPTER 37
Fast Boy

Coach Mendoza leans over me, holding an ice pack to my swelling ankle. As I focus, I hear him say, "Aha! He's coming to."

There's a wicked throbbing in my left leg; and I can feel the sticky, wet sweat covering the rest of my body. My head feels like somebody stuffed it with marshmallows.

In a rush, it all comes back: my ankle twisting, the last half mile, the last ten yards, the look on the other runner's face. My leap.

"How'd we do, Coach?" I try to sit up. "Are we in the finals?"

A huge burst of laughter showers over me, and I look around. Gathered on the grass are my dad, Mrs. Gomez, Selena, P. G., Taylor, Mark and Bryce, Aunt Laura, Uncle Jim, Kiley, and Josh.

"We won't know for sure until tomorrow, Bennett," says Coach Mendoza, "but, yeah, I think we're in the finals. In large part because of you, kid. Now, quit moving so we can get this swelling down!"

I fall back on the grass. The sky is a magnificent blue.

We did it. I didn't let the team down.

"Benny-man! I can't believe you, bro! You flew through that course!"

I smile and close my eyes, too tired to respond; but I feel the warmth of P. G.'s praise spread through my exhausted limbs.

"I always knew you were meant to be a hero, Benito," Selena teases. I smile at her and notice Taylor close by, giving Selena a once-over. I must be delirious, because I could swear she looks jealous.

"Bennett." There's only one person with a slight slur when he says the *n*'s in my name. I sit up again. My dad is grinning from ear to ear, and his eyes glisten. "You did good, son. I'm proud of you."

My heart swells. I'm proud of me, too. But hearing him say it—when only weeks ago I'd wondered if I would ever even hear him speak my name again—well, it means a lot.

"So, Bennett." Coach sits on the grass. "What in God's name were you thinking when you decided to keep running on this ankle?"

I feel a stupid grin spread across my face. I shrug, but even that hurts. "I don't know, Coach. You said if we started something, we had to finish it, right?"

"Well, you finished, kid. In seventeenth place. Just for

the record, we would have won even if you hadn't passed that last kid."

"Yeah, but we had a score to settle." I look at Mark and Bryce.

"I think you settled it." Mark smirks as he and Bryce tap knuckles.

Suddenly, I wish my mom were here. I guess I'll probably have that wish my whole life: when I graduate from high school, have my first date, move into my dorm room. I look up at the blue sky overhead.

I'm circling this date in red on my calendar, Mom, I say silently. I picture her I'm-glad-to-be-your-mom smile.

P. G. and Uncle Jim help me to my feet. I lean on them and keep my weight off my left ankle.

I limp toward the rest of my team. P. G., Bryce, and Mark shuffle alongside me.

Kendra hustles over. "Nicely done, B."

She hugs me, even though I'm all sweaty. I waggle my eyebrows at P. G., who looks more than a little envious.

While they chat about the race, I limp to my backpack and try to stay balanced while I reach down to grab it. P. G. suddenly appears and grabs it for me.

"Dude. You killed your PR! You finished in eighteen minutes and twenty-one seconds." He looks as happy as if he's run the race himself.

I look at him. My best friend since kindergarten. My trainer for the past week. "Thanks, man."

I tap his knuckles.

By the time I'm limping toward the bus, there are very few runners left milling around. Meadowbrook teachers and parents are tearing down the course. A few spectators are folding up their chairs and heading for the parking lot.

My aunt invited everyone to a celebration at her house. Josh is cooking. My dad got permission to hang out for a little while. Even Taylor is coming. That sends a weird feeling up my spine. A good weird feeling.

Up ahead is a lone Meadowbrook runner walking slowly toward the parking lot. He's a short, scrawny kid. It takes me a minute, since the sun is setting and it's blinding; but he slowly comes into focus. I realize who it is. The kid I beat at the finish line. The kid who called me Fatso.

"Hey!" I call out.

He turns around, startled. Then his eyes grow wary.

"Thanks," I say, taking a few unsteady steps toward him.

He cocks his head and glares at me.

"No, really," I say. "You gave me a good race today, and I never would have done that well if it hadn't been for you. Nice run."

I stick out my hand.

For a second he doesn't move. He looks at my hand and backs up with obvious distrust. Then, cautiously, he reaches out. He quickly shakes my hand.

"You, too," he says. Then he spins on his heel and starts jogging off.

"Bennett!" It's Coach. He's standing near the bus with his clipboard, looking impatient. "Waitin' on you, man!"

I grin. Maybe, just for today, it's okay to be last.

Acknowledgements

I'm an acknowledgments page junkie. I love reading the list of who authors choose to thank, who inspires them. I've been working on this in my head for a very long time (um, probably longer than the book itself). But the thank-you list just keeps growing....

Thanks to my agent, Jill Corcoran, for enthusiastically supporting this book from the moment we heard it was a go. Thank you to Marilyn, for being the kind of editor everyone dreams they get to work with, and for making everything about this book better than it was to start with. And my deepest gratitude to the wonderful people at Marshall Cavendish whose talents never ceased to amaze.

To the dear pre-readers who offered honest input when I needed it: Nicole Hester, the best librarian ever—no joke; Cathy Engle, whose early insight spurred me on; and my talented and supportive critique partners—Rosa Leyva, Marie Cruz, and Stephanie Denise Brown. I cherish your wisdom and your words. Many thanks also to Barbara and Rich Johnson, who graciously provided knowledge of medical insurance and guardianship. To my Spanish language consultants, Lee Ann Jackson and Abe, muchas gracias. And to Greg Morrison for being the technologically gifted "hapless soul" who agreed to do the book trailer.

Getting a book published is cool; having friends to share it with is even cooler. To the people who kept saying, "Way to go!" long after I'd passed my quota of acceptable Facebook posts: Shauntel Raymond, Therese Lowrie, Lisa Elofson, Shawnee Huss, Jennifer Hoey, Fran Arriaga, Melissa Haines, among many others.

I wrote this book because, as a coach, I'm continually inspired by runners—young and old. Eddie and Faith Rosas; Ed, Katie, Mike, and Emily Lowrie—to you and the many former, current, and future runners at Goddard Middle School: thank you for making cross country a sport of which I'm proud to be a part.

And finally, the biggest thank you possible to my family. Tom, Linda, and Sherri—your enthusiasm for this dream-come-true touches my heart. Mom and Dad—for always cheering; I am beyond lucky to have you. Josh, your encouragement and interest in this process has meant the world. And Brad—you read this story (even though the whole thing is made up) and you never doubted that others would someday read it, too. Thank you for still being the guy I want to tell first.

Zach, Jake, and Molly—I'll be forever grateful that you took this journey with me; your excitement makes being your mom the best job ever.